'What are you thinking about?'

Anna blinked. 'Oh—something that happened at the weekend, that's all.'

'It must have been pretty good—you were all misty-eyed.'

She laughed self-consciously, not ready to tell this stranger about her little Flissy. Men had a way of judging a single mother, and Anna wasn't ready to be judged by this man.

Not judged and found wanting.

Kids. . .one of life's joys, one of life's treasures.

Kisses. . .of warmth, kisses of passion, kisses from mothers and kisses from lovers.

In *Kids & Kisses*. . .every story has it all.

Caroline Anderson's nursing career was brought to an abrupt halt by a back injury, but her interest in medical things led her to work first as a medical secretary, and then after completing her teacher training, as a lecturer in Medical Office Practice to trainee medical secretaries. In addition to writing, she also runs her own business from her home in rural Suffolk, where she lives with her husband, two daughters, mother and assorted animals.

Recent titles by the same author:

TAKEN FOR GRANTED
ANYONE CAN DREAM
ONCE MORE, WITH FEELING
NOTHING LEFT TO GIVE

LOVE WITHOUT MEASURE

BY
CAROLINE ANDERSON

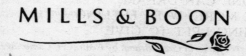

MILLS & BOON

MILLS & BOON, the Rose Device and LOVE ON CALL
are trademarks of the publisher.
Harlequin Mills & Boon Limited,
Eton House, 18–24 Paradise Road, Richmond, Surrey TW9 1SR
This edition published by arrangement with
Harlequin Enterprises B.V.

© Caroline Anderson 1995

ISBN 0 263 79096 7

Set in 10 on 11 pt Linotron Times
03-9507-55484

Typeset in Great Britain by CentraCet, Cambridge
Made and printed in Great Britain

CHAPTER ONE

ANNA heard his laugh first, a deep, rich chuckle that
made the corners of her mouth curl involuntarily and
softened the lines of tiredness around her eyes.

Laughter could convey many things, she thought—
happiness, amusement, joy, even scorn and derision.
This man's laugh was sheer enjoyment, full of warmth
and humour. It was the laugh of a man glad to be alive,
and she sensed he was also comfortable, a man at ease
with himself and the world.

It was also a big laugh, and she knew before she
turned the corner that his body would match it. Even
so, her first sight of him made her breath catch, and
she faltered.

He was tall, his body lean and rangy, with wide,
square shoulders and long legs; he was leaning against
the wall, his white coat held back by the hands thrust
deep into his trouser pockets, amply displaying his
narrow hips and taut, flat stomach. One knee was bent
and the sole of his shoe was propped casually against
the wall at mid-calf.

He was deep in conversation with Jack Lawrence,
the A and E unit consultant, and as she watched his
mouth opened again and his head tipped back. The
laugh rippled round her again, and she felt a shiver
start deep inside. Who was he?

The new senior registrar, she realised. Patrick something. At least he looked confident. They had been
plagued by a recent houseman who had been a total
pain, and losing their previous and excellent SR Ben
Bradshaw to an unknown quantity could have been

5

very bad news. Hopefully this guy would pass muster, as a doctor anyway. As a man, there was no question.

She forced herself to walk towards them, confused by the sudden speeding of her heart. This was crazy—he was just a colleague! Probably, please, God, safely married like Ben.

He looked completely relaxed and thoroughly at home, which was quite remarkable considering he had only started on the unit ten minutes ago. That laugh found its way up from his throat again, teasing the air with its joyful sound. Anna's mouth curved involuntarily.

As she approached Jack looked up with a smile and held out his arm towards her, drawing her into their circle.

'Anna, I want you to meet Patrick Haddon, our new SR. Patrick, this is Staff Nurse Anna Jarvis, Kathleen's second in command.'

He shrugged away from the wall, standing straight at last, so she could see how large he really was, and took his hands out of his pockets as he turned towards her.

The light caught the dull gleam of a gold band on the ring-finger of his left hand, and her breath eased out in a sigh of relief—relief that felt curiously like disappointment. He was married. She was conscious of the silly smile still lurking round her mouth, and forced it into a smile of welcome. His own mouth tipped into an answering grin, and she felt something kick under her ribs. 'Hi,' she managed, a touch breathlessly.

She took the proferred hand, noting almost absently its dry warmth and firm grip. It was his eyes which had her attention, though; they were a warm, deep brown, rich and full of humour, and yet still gentle. She had the feeling he could see into her soul. It was a most uncomfortable sensation, and yet curiously she didn't feel threatened. It was only uncomfortable because it was so unexpected.

'Hello, Anna,' he said quietly, and his voice seemed to resonate deep inside her, rippling out into the cold, quiet reaches of her loneliness.

No! He was married! She dropped his hand, the contact suddenly too much to cope with. 'Welcome aboard, Dr Haddon,' she replied, managing to find the social niceties despite the strange sensations in the pit of her stomach. She turned towards the other man. 'Jack, have you seen Kathleen?'

'She's in the end cubicle with a fracture. If you go and give her a hand I'll be along in a minute, once I've sorted Patrick out.'

'Thanks.' She turned and walked away, conscious of those searching eyes following her. The hair on the back of her neck prickled, and she had to force herself not to run.

As she turned into the cubicle she risked a glance back. He was still watching her, his eyes steady, a thoughtful look on his face.

She went behind the curtain, her heart thumping. Not a flirt, she prayed. Please, God, not a flirt. Sexual harassment was the one thing Anna hated above all else, particularly when it came in the form of a flirting playboy, and most especially when he was married. She found herself feeling suddenly sorry for the wife she had dreamed up for him.

How must it feel to catch a man like that just to discover he was a will-o'-the-wisp? She dismissed the memory of those eyes, far from flirting, just gently assessing, and seeing far too much for her peace of mind. She would think of him as a flirt. That way he would be easily dismissed, pushed to the back of her mind, not worth the time of day.

Kathleen looked up from the trousers she was easing off and smiled. 'Good morning, Staff.'

'Morning, Sister. Do you need a hand?'

'Oh, yes, please. This is Mr James. He fell off the kerb, didn't you?'

The man nodded and winced. 'Right down a pothole. Teach me to look where I'm going, won't it? Are you sure you shouldn't cut those trousers?'

Kathleen laughed. 'And have you sueing me for a new pair? Don't worry, I'll be careful.'

'You'd better be,' he muttered, grim-lipped, and subsided on to the pillow with a groan. Together Anna and Kathleen eased the trousers down, slipped his good foot out, and carefully removed them from the damaged one without even making him wince.

Perversely he looked disappointed, and Anna almost laughed.

The skin was very scraped, and Anna could see his foot was lying at a strange angle. Kathleen straightened up and smiled.

'I'll get a doctor to come and have a look at you, Mr James, while Staff Nurse Jarvis cleans you up a bit more.'

'They're in the corridor. Jack's just coming,' Anna told her, and Kathleen nodded and went out quietly through the curtain.

'This looks very sore,' Anna said as she pulled on gloves and cleaned the skin a little. 'Am I hurting you?'

'It is rather tender,' he said a bit stiffly, and Anna stopped as soon as she had wiped away the worst of the blood and dirt from around his graze. It was obvious that the fibula was broken, so he would probably need an anaesthetic to set the bone and there was no point in torturing him for the hell of it. Whoever examined him could see enough now.

The curtain swished beside her, and she felt a shiver

run over her skin. She didn't need to look to know it wasn't Jack Lawrence. Gorgeous though he was, his magnetism was strictly limited to Kathleen. This man, though. . .

'Mr James? I'm Dr Haddon. I gather you've hurt you leg—mind if I have a look?'

'Be my guest.'

He bent his head over the leg, checked the foot for warmth and sensation, and then tutted quietly. 'It looks a bit nasty, doesn't it? I think we need an X-ray first, to assess the extent of the damage, but I'm pretty sure you've just broken the bone at the side of your leg— the fibula. You may have damaged some of the bones in your foot as well, but the X-ray will pick that up. Whatever, you'll need an operation to fix that bone properly, I'm afraid.'

The man sighed heavily. 'Can't you just put a plaster on it?'

Patrick shook his head. 'Sorry. It won't heal unless we can pull the bone-ends into alignment, and that will need surgery, I'm almost sure.'

'Damn. I'm supposed to be flying to America tomorrow.'

'Well, I'm sorry, you won't be going—not for a good while.'

He swore, softly but fluently. 'I have to go,' he repeated.

'Sorry, old chap, that's the way it goes,' Patrick told him calmly.

It didn't calm him noticeably. 'I've got my mobile phone here—do you mind if I make some calls while I wait?' he asked, already flicking up the aerial.

'Be our guest,' Patrick told him, and, making sure the sides were up on the examination couch, Anna followed him out to fill in the X-ray request forms and get Patrick to authorise them.

Behind them they could hear Mr James's voice on the phone.

'Fallen off the pavement and broken my goddamn leg—what? I said I fell off the bloody pavement!' he yelled.

Patrick grinned at Anna. 'Oops. I think our business executive's heading for a mid-life crisis,' he said softly, and she chuckled despite her intentions to have nothing to do with him.

He followed her into the office, perched on the edge of the desk so that his lean, well-muscled thigh was just inches from her hand, and watched as she made a total foul up of the first form.

'Damn,' she muttered, and, screwing it up, she lobbed it towards the bin and missed.

'Calm down. You're getting like Alan James.'

She snorted, but tackled the next form slowly. 'There—could you sign, please?'

His hands were fascinating—tanned, the backs lightly scattered with dark hair, the fingers strong and straight. She forced herself to look at the ring on his left hand, to remind herself that he was married.

That was when she saw the scar, a jagged white line that ran from thumb to wrist. She found herself touching it before she knew what she was doing.

'What happened?' she asked.

He glanced at it dismissively. 'I don't know. I was helping at an earthquake, pulling rubble off the remains of a school.'

'An earthquake?'

'Mmm. Here, he can go through now.'

She took the form, clearly dismissed, and went and wheeled Mr James through to X-ray, trying not to let idle curiosity distract her from her job. Except that earthquakes in this country were rarer than hen's teeth. . .

Mr James was still on the phone. Grudgingly he put it down and subsided to a steady grumble for the X-ray. Sure enough, it was a clean fracture of the fibula with no other damage to the foot, but it would need plating to draw it back into alignment.

As she wheeled him back to the cubicle Nick Davidson, the orthopaedic SR on take, appeared and walked towards them with a grin.

'Is this my patient?'

'Yup—here are the plates, and this is Mr James.'

Nick introduced himself and shook the man's hand. 'My name's Davidson. I'm the orthopaedic surgeon who's going to be fixing this. Shall we have a look?'

He thrust the plates up into the light-box and grunted, then pointed to the broken ends of the bone, explaining to Mr James what he was going to do. 'When did you last eat?'

'Last night.'

'No breakfast?'

'I never have time.'

'Good—this once. When did you drink last?'

'Coffee at eight before I left home.'

Nick glanced at his watch. 'Nine thirty-five. OK, we'll take you up to the ward and prep you, and I'll tack you on the end of my list. You'll go to Theatre just before lunch, OK?'

'If it's really necessary,' he grumbled.

'It's really necessary.'

He snorted. 'I've got more calls to make—can I have a private room?'

'Only if there's a single room free at the time. Ask the staff on the ward.'

He left, and Mr James stared after him. 'Is that it?'

Anna was astonished. 'What did you want him to say?'

'I want to know when I'll be up and about—when can I leave hospital?'

She stuck her head out of the curtains and called after Nick. 'Mr James wants to know when he can leave hospital.'

Nick turned, walking backwards down the corridor as he spoke. 'Whenever he feels ready,' he called back. 'I suspect about a week. Then he'll need two weeks at least with it up, and another week or two slowly mobilising. Five to six before he's walking regularly with crutches. And no, he can't fly tomorrow.'

She went back into the cubicle. 'Did you hear that?'

'Bloody ridiculous,' he growled. 'Is he a consultant?'

Anna took a steadying breath. 'No, he's a senior registrar.'

'I want to see the big cheese—I'm not going to be fobbed off with some incompetent junior doctor.'

She hung on to her temper with difficulty. 'I can assure you, Mr Davidson isn't a junior doctor, nor is he incompetent! His next post will be a consultancy— probably in the fairly near future. And he's more than qualified to mend your ankle!'

Mr James was stubbornly unrepentant. 'I want it done privately,' he stated. 'I don't have time to mess about like this.'

She eyed him with disfavour. 'Could you explain something to me? Would you tell me how paying for it is going to make your leg heal any quicker?'

'I might get better treatment,' he grumbled. 'At least a real specialist. I can't afford to take weeks off,' he added petulantly.

'You should have thought of that when you weren't looking where you were going, shouldn't you?' she said sweetly, and with that she swished out into the corridor smack into a laughing Patrick Haddon.

She glared at him, but he winked and took her arm, leading her away.

'Calm down,' he soothed, and led her into the staff-room, pressing a cup of coffee into her hand. 'Drink this. There's nothing requiring your immediate attention, so take a little time out and relax.'

She snorted. 'Pompous ass. I don't suppose there's the slightest chance he'll get pneumonia from the anaesthetic?'

Patrick laughed again, his eyes creased with delight. 'You're a wicked woman.'

'Only when provoked, and boy, did that man provoke me!' She sipped her coffee, then sighed. 'Oh, this is luxury. What a nasty shock, coming back to that after a wonderful weekend!'

'What do you expect—gratitude? This is the great British public. We're here to serve them, and do it on time, regardless of what might have just gone on behind the scenes.'

She stared at him. 'You sound really bitter.'

'Do I?' He gave a quick grin. 'Sorry. I've been in Africa for the last two years. They queue up there for days to see you, and never complain. Mostly they're too weak, but they're pathetically grateful for any slight kindness. It's very humbling.'

The weary smile didn't reach his eyes. 'Sorry. Don't let me get on my hobby-horse. I'm back here now, and I should just accept the absurd plethora of medical equipment and facilities instead of begrudging it to these miserable ingrates.'

His smile robbed his words of any offence, and Anna found herself even more curious about him. If he felt so passionately about Africa, why come home? Now was not the time to ask him, though, because he was still speaking, asking for her help.

'Sit down for a minute,' he suggested. 'I could do

with being filled in on procedure, names, places—that
sort of thing. Who do I call, who do I avoid, who's got
a tetchy temper?—apart from you, of course.'

His smile took the criticism out of his words, and she
found herself smiling back.

'I'm normally very calm, but when someone questions a colleague's competence, and says they'd get
better treatment if they paid for it, I get very, very
cross.'

'Let him pay. It relieves the stress on the hospital's
funds. Anyway, you shouldn't get so worked up. You'll
get ulcers.'

'No, I won't. Not if I haven't got Helicobacter
pylori.'

'Smart-mouth.'

There was no malice in his remark, and they shared
a smile.

'Thanks for the coffee.'

She dropped into a chair and sighed. The weekend
had been hectic, and already seemed a long way away.
Flissy had been dancing in her ballet class, and Anna
had had to dress her and pile her wispy hair up into a
bun, and then watch the tiny little scrap trip and dither
her way across the room, pretending to be a butterfly.

A virtuoso performance it wasn't, but it had reduced
Anna to a sniffling, pink-eyed heap. Pride was a
ridiculous thing, she thought.

'What are you thinking about?'

She blinked. 'Oh—nothing. Something that happened at the weekend, that's all.'

'It must have been pretty good—you were all misty-
eyed.'

She laughed self-consciously, not ready to tell this
stranger about her little Flissy. Men had a way of
judging a single mother, and Anna wasn't ready to be
judged by this man. Not judged and found wanting.

'It was good,' she said, and deliberately changed the subject. 'So, tell me about Africa. Was that where the earthquake was?'

A shadow crossed his eyes. 'No,' he said, effectively cutting off the conversation.

She blinked. So he, too, had things he wasn't prepared to talk about.

She studied her cup, swirling the dregs of her coffee round and wondering why he was suddenly so remote and cut off. Had someone he loved died in the earthquake? Perhaps a wife or child? Oh, God, not a child! He'd said it was a school. . .

'You didn't lose someone—not your child?' she asked, unable to help herself.

He met her eyes, his own revealing a flash of pain. 'No,' he agreed quietly. 'Not my child.'

But someone. What was the saying about fools rushing in? Her shoulders drooped. 'Look, I'm sorry I dragged the whole thing up——'

She jerked to her feet, almost dropping her cup back on the table, and fled.

She heard him call her name, but she didn't stop. She went out to the front desk, glanced round, and picked up the notes for a patient who had just arrived.

'Mrs Lucas? Would you like to come with me, please?'

He caught up with her at lunchtime, when she was just grabbing ten minutes for another coffee and a biscuit.

'Is that all you're having?' he asked in disbelief.

'I don't eat much during the day,' she told him, unprepared to get into discussion about it.

'You can't work as hard as you have been on that. Come and have some lunch with me—we never did have that conversation. I'll offend someone mortally, and it will be your fault. Do you really want that on your conscience?'

His smile was warm and teasing. He was clearly quite unbothered about offending anyone. He wasn't the offensive sort. He also wasn't the sort to be thwarted.

'Come on, while it's quiet.'

She shook her head, reminding herself that he was married. 'No. I really don't want to go to the canteen.'

'Then it will come to you. Wait here.'

He left the room, his long legs eating up the corridor. She heard the quiet swish of the door as he left the department, and, shutting her eyes, she leant her head back with a sigh. She felt like King Canute—totally helpless in the face of such stubborn determination. It would be easier to give in, but she didn't want to. That would give him the upper hand, and absolutely the last thing she needed was to be bullied by a man, especially somebody else's husband. . .

'You sound tired.'

She opened her eyes. 'Hello, Kath. No, I'm not tired, I'm saving my energy. Our Dr Haddon has decided I need to eat more. I think I'm about to be force-fed.'

Kath laughed, the action declaring her on Patrick's side. 'Good job, too,' she retorted. 'You're far too skinny.' She helped herself to coffee and dropped into a chair next to Anna, kicking off her shoes and rubbing her toes. 'So, what do you think of him?'

Anna shrugged non-committally. 'He seems very competent.'

Kath laughed. 'Competent? He's big, Anna—B-I-G. Just what we need to sit on all the drunks while we wrestle them into submission. Ben was fine, but he just didn't have Patrick's weight, and Jack's not always here.'

Anna swallowed. Patrick was big, true, but size

armour. He looked about thirty-five, she thought, maybe younger, but his face had that lived-in look that had seen many sides of life, not all of them kind. The earthquake? Perhaps that had aged him. He was good-looking, though. Good bone-structure, his body broad and strong without being overly heavy. There wasn't an ounce of fat on him, she thought, despite his prodigious appetite. He bit into another sandwich and glanced up, meeting her eyes. His mouth occupied, he waved instead at the food.

'More,' he mumbled.

'I couldn't.'

'Fruit, then—or a doughnut.'

She felt herself weaken. 'You've got doughnuts?' she asked hopefully. 'Are they warm?'

He nodded, his mouth busy again.

'Jam?'

He nodded, the corners of his eyes crinkled with understanding.

She heard her stomach rumble. Oh, what the heck? He clearly intended to feed her till she split. She couldn't disappoint him.

The doughnut was wonderful, light and fluffy, the jam still warm. It squirted down her chin and she laughed and reached for a tissue.

He was there first, a napkin at the ready, steadying her jaw with his other hand as he wiped the jam away. Their eyes met, and for a long and almost unbearable second she thought he was going to kiss her.

Then he sat back, cobbling up the napkin and lobbing it neatly into the bin.

Her breath eased slowly out. Had she imagined it? Oh, God.

She finished the doughnut and then wiped her fingers, reaching for her coffee with hands that were not quite steady. She cast about for another topic for her mind, and came up with money as the safest option.

'What do I owe you for that lot?' she asked.

He looked astonished. 'Owe me? Nothing.'

'Don't be silly, it must have cost a fortune.'

'I think I can just about run to a few sandwiches for our first date,' he said drily, and drained his coffee-cup while she tried to ignore the funny hiccup in her heartbeat at his use of the word 'date'. Ridiculous. 'However,' he continued, 'if you insist on going Dutch you can refill my cup, bring me a banana, and tell me everything I need to know to keep out of trouble.'

Clearly it was as far as she was going to get. 'Are you always this stubborn and bossy?' she asked mildly as she did as she was told.

'Always. Thank you.' He took the cup and set it down. 'Now, the trade-off. Who do I have to avoid, who do I have to crawl to, what are the internal politics?'

She groaned. 'Internal politics? I try and stay out of it. Funding, of course, is always a hassle. So far they haven't threatened to close us down, but funding for our emergency teams going out to incidents is always a bit of a fraught issue. They say it's very expensive, and I'm sure it is, but it's absolutely vital that we continue to keep the service available and I'm sure in the long run we actually save money.'

He nodded. 'Who usually goes?'

'The most senior members of staff available to a small incident. To a major incident with multiple casualties we usually keep several senior staff here to deal with the casualties as they come in, but others, of course, go out for on-the-spot surgery and emergency resuscitation. The first job in major incidents is Triage, really, sorting the patients into priority for transfer to hospital, and that's something we're all very used to.'

'Do you have a Triage system operating in the unit all the time?' he asked.

Anna nodded. 'Yes—it's often me doing that. We only bother if it gets busy, but the reception staff are excellent and keep us in touch all the time with what's coming through the door.'

Patrick stretched out, his long legs crossed at the ankle, and balanced his coffee-cup on his chest. 'What's the usual waiting-time?'

She laughed softly. 'You tell me. Certainly less than several days, unlike your Africa. We try and keep it down to under half an hour, and patients are always seen by the Triage nurse within a few minutes of arrival in any case, unless we're so quiet that they're virtually straight in. Sometimes, though, it can be up to an hour before they get seen and that really bothers me. It's the malingerers that mess up the system—the people that won't go to their GP because they don't like to bother him, or because they have to wait in the surgery, or because this is more convenient than trying to get an appointment. Last week we had a man who came in with piles.'

'They can be very painful,' Patrick said reasonably. 'He might well have been worried, especially if they were bleeding.'

'They weren't,' she retorted, 'and he'd had them twenty years!'

Patrick chuckled. 'So who had the pleasure of telling him where to go?'

'Kathleen—and very effective she was, too! She has a pet thing about people who abuse the system. She asked him if he'd left his glasses behind, and pointed out the sign. "Have you had an accident?" she asked. "Is it an emergency?" He left quite quickly.'

'I'll bet. She's a little fire-cracker, I should think.'

Anna smiled indulgently. 'She can be. She's also very gentle and kind.'

'And married to the boss, of course.'

'Oh, yes. They can be quite nauseating.'

He chuckled. 'Really?'

'Really, although you'd think they'd have grown out of it by now. They've been married nearly eighteen months.'

'Nah, they're still newly-weds,' he said with another of his infectious chuckles. He tipped his coffee-cup and she watched his very masculine throat work as he swallowed. Then he stretched luxuriously, totally unselfconscious, and hauled himself to his feet.

'I suppose we ought to let the love-birds go to lunch and do some work,' he said with a smile. 'There's still some food left—want another doughnut?'

She shook her head. 'No. I won't need to eat again for days.'

He snorted rudely, grabbed a sandwich as they passed the table, and headed towards the cubicles.

Stifling a smile, Anna followed.

A few minutes later she lost all urge to smile.

A message came from ambulance control to say that a young boy, Simeon Wilding, was being brought in direct from school with a severe asthma attack, and he was reported to be in a serious condition.

'OK,' Patrick said calmly. 'We'll take him straight into Crash. Can someone clear it, please, and get it ready? We may need to ventilate him. Any information on drugs?'

Anna shook her head. 'No, nothing. He's a known asthmatic; we may have the notes. Julie's searching for them.'

Julie was the receptionist, and, having checked for notes held in the unit, would then check with the asthma clinic. If they were in the hospital, Julie would track them down in the next few minutes.

Until then, they just had to play it by ear. They prepared the nebuliser with salbutamol, cleared the decks and waited.

They heard the ambulance coming and went to the door in time to see it sweep in very rapidly. The doors were flung open and the boy was out, heading for the department, with Patrick running beside the trolley and examining the lad as they came.

Anna could see that his lips were blue, his eyes wide, and he was clearly fighting for breath. Then, as she watched, his eyes closed and he stopped breathing.

Patrick swore, very softly, and yanked down the blanket, slapping the stethoscope on his chest as they manoeuvred through the doors.

'Damn. He's arrested. Get him into Crash.'

They ran, leaving him on the trolley for speed as they all went automatically into action as soon as the trolley was stationary.

Feeling for the breastbone, Patrick crossed his hands and pumped hard on the boy's chest.

Anna heard a dull creak and winced. A rib had gone. Oh, well, it was better than dying. She didn't have time to think about it, though, because she had to take over from Patrick while he inserted the cuffed tube and blew it up, sealing the airway. Then he connected it to the humidified air from the ventilator unit on the wall and watched as the boy's chest rose and fell.

They alternated cardiac massage with positive ventilation, to allow the air to be forced into his lungs, together with a measured dose of a bronchodilator to combat the swollen tubes in his lungs that were preventing him from breathing.

While Anna worked another nurse was putting monitor leads on his chest, and then he was connected up and they could see the flat trace that indicated the heart was still not beating.

'Damn you, don't you dare die,' Patrick muttered, and, pushing Anna out of the way, he thumped the boy's chest hard.

The line wiggled, then settled into an erratic rhythm. 'He's fibrillating—I'll give him a jolt. Stand back, everyone, please.'

They took a pace back while Patrick held the paddles to the boy's chest. 'Shock, please,' Patrick said.

The boy's body arched and flopped, and the trace suddenly corrected itself. As it did, the boy's lips turned less blue and he started to fidget.

'I'll give him a minute and then we'll try him off the ventilator,' Patrick told them, and bent over the boy.

'Simeon, it's OK, you're going to be fine,' he said calmly, his voice reassuring.

The boy's eyelids fluttered up and he started to fight the ventilator. Patrick disconnected him from the machine and watched to see if he could breathe alone. To their relief his chest rose and fell gently. 'Good,' Patrick said, and, letting down the cuff, he withdrew the endotracheal tube from the boy's mouth.

He coughed, his breath rasping, and Anna replaced the tube with a mask connected to a nebuliser. Warm, damp air flowed into his lungs, and within minutes he looked much better.

'My chest hurts—I want my mum,' he said in a small voice, and beside her Anna felt Patrick almost sag with relief. He was all right; the fight for air had been won before it was too late. Another few seconds and he could have suffered irreversible brain damage.

Even so, Patrick was worried about him.

'I think he ought to go into ITU for a day or so, if the paediatrician agrees,' he said quietly to Anna.

She nodded. It was standard procedure to over-protect their young asthmatic patients, because attacks of that severity rarely happened in isolation and in ITU everything necessary was there at hand.

The paediatric consultant, Andrew Barrett, arrived then and took over, examining the boy and chatting quietly to him.

It seemed they were old friends—the boy a frequent visitor to the paediatric ward. This time, though, Andrew agreed with Patrick. It had been a little too close for comfort, and they were erring on the safe side.

Just as he left the department Jack and Kathleen Lawrence came back in, staring at the trolley in surprise.

'Was that Simeon Wilding?'

'Yes—asthma attack. He arrested,' Patrick told them economically.

'What?' Jack looked shocked.

Patrick smiled slightly. 'He's OK—well, apart from a rib I may have cracked. He's going to Paediatric ITU for a couple of days, just to be on the safe side. He stopped breathing, but he's spoken to us and he's OK—at least for now.'

Jack's mouth tipped into a cynical curve. 'Of course he is—after all, it's only asthma.'

Anna heard the bitterness in his voice and under-stood it. Asthma was so common that it tended to be ignored, underestimated, almost brushed aside until a crisis forced it into view.

An event like this brought you up hard against reality, she thought. Most of their critical asthmatics made it, but every now and again they would lose a patient to it, even though it was 'only asthma'.

They all felt so helpless then, and Jack hated being

helpless. Patrick, too, she realised, looking at them as they shared a frustrated smile.

'Oh, well, we do what we can. Well done for saving him,' Jack said, and rested his hand on Patrick's shoulder.

'I've been meaning to give you a guided tour of the department all morning—but I guess you've seen Crash now?'

Patrick laughed. 'Yes—thank you.'

'How about a coffee?' Kathleen suggested.

Just then the phone rang, and as one they all turned to look at it, then shrugged.

'So who needed coffee anyway?' Kathleen said philosophically, and picked up the phone.

CHAPTER TWO

PATRICK stood up to leave. The elderly man in the chair by the window regarded him without curiosity.

'Are you going now?' he asked.

'Yes. I'll see you tomorrow.'

The old boy shook his head. 'Very kind of you, I'm sure, but I can't see why you should want to.'

Patrick quelled the pain. 'Would you rather I didn't come?' he asked quietly.

'Oh, no. I enjoy your company, young fella. Too many old girls in this place for my liking. No, I was thinking of you. I just can't see the attraction in talking to an old codger like me.'

Patrick smiled, a sad half-smile that didn't reach his eyes.

'I find you very interesting. You've had a fascinating life.'

The man snorted. 'You must have a very boring life, young man, if you find mine fascinating. Very boring.'

Patrick thought back over the last few years, and gave a wry, quiet laugh. 'It's quite exciting enough for me. I'll see you tomorrow.'

They shook hands formally, and Patrick turned to leave. As he did so the man called him back.

'Patrick?' he said.

He turned towards him again. 'Yes?'

'I don't know who you are, young man, but I'd be proud if you *were* my son.'

Patrick's face twisted slightly. 'Thank you,' he said softly. 'Thank you very much. Goodnight.'

He went out, waving a greeting at the sister who was

27

busy wheeling another resident through the grounds, and slipped behind the wheel of his car—his father's car, in fact.

For a moment he remained motionless, letting the pain ease away, giving himself time. Then he started the car and drove back to the lovely Tudor house where he had grown up, and where he was now staying with his mother.

She was in the front garden when he pulled up, and she straightened and went to greet him with a kiss. 'How was he?' she asked.

Patrick shrugged. 'The same.'

'Still doesn't know you?'

He shook his head. His eyes blurred, fogging his vision, and he blinked hard. 'I miss him,' he said unevenly.

'So do I,' his mother said sadly. 'Oh, Patrick, I'm so glad you're home.'

They hugged each other, drawing comfort from the contact, sharing their sorrow. The lump in Patrick's throat grew, and he eased away.

'I'll put the car in the garage, then I need to change.'

'Don't be long. I want to hear all about your day.'

He didn't doubt it. He put the car away and went in through the side door into the converted stable-block that had been turned into a self-contained annexe for guests. He had refused to stay in the house with his mother, preferring instead to maintain his independence and privacy while still being close at hand.

Now, as he stripped in the airy bedroom and wandered through to the little bathroom to shower, he was glad he had insisted. He needed room to himself, a little time and space to be quiet and recharge his batteries.

And God knows they were flat enough. This sudden deterioration of his father's was the last straw, the

Alzheimer's that had been creeping up now claiming his memory and distancing him from the son who had travelled back across half the world to be near him.

A heavy sadness settled in Patrick's chest, joining the other weight that lay there at all times, ignored for the most part but omnipresent, a constant anchor round his heart.

He turned on the shower and stood under the hot, stinging spray, his eyes closed, letting the water pelt over him and wash away the smell of the nursing-home.

Ideally he would like to bring his father home, but his mother couldn't cope alone now her husband was incontinent. Perhaps, with Patrick's help and the services of an agency nurse, it would be possible.

He would consider it, talk it over with his mother.

Half an hour later he joined her in the conservatory overlooking the garden that had been his father's pride and joy. It was a mess, the weeds forming a mat between the perennials, the vegetable patch untended. Patrick had cut the grass at the weekend but already it seemed to be growing. His mother did what she could, but there was too much for one person to look after. They needed a gardener.

He sighed and picked up the wine his mother had poured him, raising it to his lips. It was cold and crisp, rinsing away the strain of the day.

'So—tell me about your new job,' his mother began, tucking her feet under her bottom like a girl and leaning eagerly towards him. 'What are the rest of the staff like? Are you going to be happy working there?'

He thought of Jack Lawrence, his boss—apparently casual and yet with a mind like a steel trap, decisive and efficient. Kathleen, his wife, a softly-spoken little Irishwoman with a spark in her eye and a core of iron.

And Anna.

Something unfamiliar and forgotten happened in his chest, a sort of tightening, a feeling of anticipation.

She was no oil-painting, their little staff nurse. Not that little, really, unless she was beside him, then she seemed unbelievably fragile, with her wide grey eyes and clear, almost transparent skin. Her hair was long, he guessed. It was hard to tell with it twisted up under her cap, but certainly shoulder-length at least, and a wonderful dark brown, like polished mahogany. She wasn't really pretty, but there was a life in her, an inner beauty that transcended her slightly uneven features and made her if anything even more attractive.

She was too thin, of course. Kathleen had implied that no one took care of her. Certainly she didn't take care of herself. The way she had fallen on those sandwiches——

'Well?'

He blinked. 'Um. . .'

'I asked about your colleagues, and you went into a trance.'

He grinned easily at his mother. 'Sorry, I was thinking about the day. Yes, they're fine. A good bunch of people. I think I'm going to enjoy working there.'

His mother sipped her wine and regarded him steadily. 'Are you going to tell me about the woman who put that look in your eye, or are you going to keep me guessing?'

He could feel the flush on the back of his neck. 'Woman?' he said casually.

His mother sighed. 'You're going to keep me guessing. OK.'

'Whatever makes you think there's a woman?' he asked with feigned amusement.

'Patrick!' The gently teasing reproof undid him. He never could hide anything from his mother.

in such comparatively good condition. He'd been trapped by several tons of steel across his chest and pelvis, and when they had lifted it away his leg had been lying beside his arm, bent up courtesy of his shattered pelvis.

And shattered it most certainly was. A large part of his hipbone was detached and lying oddly, and the bones which formed the bowl of the pelvis were broken on both sides at the front and on the right at the back. As a result his whole pelvis was grossly unstable.

As if that wasn't enough, both femurs were fractured, the right in two places, and his left hip was dislocated. In short, he was a mess.

Nick Davidson was on his way down from Theatre to see the plates, and it was likely the man would go straight there for emergency surgery to fix his pelvis and femurs. In preparation for such an event they had taken blood for cross-matching already, and were running in Haemacel to replace the massive blood-loss caused by his fractures. Whether there was any other damage was unclear as yet, but he was being closely watched. It was hard to tell from the circulatory loss alone, because fractures of that order caused such massive blood-loss that abdominal injuries could easily go undetected.

Nick wandered in as they stood frowning at the X-rays, and rested a hand on each of their shoulders. 'Hi, folks. This my customer?'

'Yup.' Patrick filled him in, and Nick winced.

'Sounds nasty.'

'It is.'

He studied the plates quietly, then pursed his lips.

'We can't do it all at once. I'll get a fixator on to hold it all a bit steady, but he'll need plating and pinning once the bleeding has settled at the fracture sites. I'll have to do the femurs today, though. Any abdominal damage apart from the pelvis?'

'No evidence of any. He's in very good shape really—in pain, of course. We've given him Entonox gas, because his circulation is too close to collapse to risk diamorphine, but it isn't really anything like enough.'

'It won't be,' Nick agreed. 'We'll soon knock him out. What about blood?'

'He's been cross-matched and we're boosting his circulation as fast as we can. We'll be able to do more when we get the whole blood.'

Nick nodded. 'OK, I'll have a word with him and then we'll get him up to Theatre. Has he signed the consent form?'

'He's not in that good shape,' Anna said drily. 'His wife's here—I'll get her to do that.'

'Thanks. Right, where is he?'

Anna left them with the patient and went into the office.

Nick joined her a few minutes later. 'All done?'

She nodded. 'His wife's signed. She'd like to see him before he goes up to Theatre.'

'I'll go and find her. Give me the forms, I'll take them with me.'

He headed off towards the waiting-room, X-rays and forms in hand, and Anna watched him go. Another gorgeous hunk, one that half the hospital were apparently in love with, including most specifically his wife Cassie, the only scrub-nurse he would tolerate and who would tolerate him, so rumour had it.

His temper in Theatre was legendary, but his results were astonishing and he was tipped for stardom. It made her laugh that Mr James had queried his competence. He was probably the most skilful and intuitive orthopaedic surgeon in the hospital, bar none.

And yet he left her cold. No, not cold, she acknowledged, just warmed with admiration and a genuine liking.

Whereas Patrick——!

How had he managed to break through her reserve and reach that part of her so carefully guarded that even she scarcely knew it existed?

But break through it he had, and now her skin shivered when he approached, her heart beat faster, and when he looked at her with those melting brown eyes her insides turned to mush.

And when he touched her. . .! Even an accidental brushing of his hand against hers made her heart race and her skin heat. She was like a teenager, anticipating her first kiss. Her breath caught in her throat at the image that provoked, and she rolled her eyes in self-disgust. If it hadn't been so worrying it would have been laughable.

But she was worried. She was too vulnerable, too inexperienced to deal with a sexy, meaningless flirta-tion—or, worse still, a casual affair with a married man.

Her heart thumped at the thought, and her mind recalled with absolute clarity the vivid dream she had had the night before.

Her cheeks heated at the memory, and she quickly busied herself with the admission details for Nick's patient, Clive Ronson. How she had managed such a provocative dream anyway, she didn't know. She had no experience of any of the moves he had made, or any of the feelings she had quite definitely felt!

She cobbled up the form and tried again.

Patrick was cross with himself. He was trying to write up notes and all he could think about was the feel of Anna's body beside his as they had worked together on Clive Ronson. She was too thin, he thought critically, but still she managed to stir him. The jut of her hip was still unmistakeably feminine, the brush of her thigh like the soft stroke of fire against his leg as she had leant across to cut away the patient's trousers. He had been in her way, and yet a perverse part of him had refused to move.

He wanted her.

It shocked him, the realisation that she was capable of getting past the ice around his heart and setting his body on fire like this.

It was only physical, he knew that. It could never be anything more meaningful, but that didn't diminish its power. Oh, no. Almost the reverse. Because it was just sex, just meaningless, hot, physical lust, his mind could allow it.

His body was helpless. He shifted uncomfortably, embarrassingly aware of the heavy heat that suffused him, the very present evidence of his desire.

He glanced down at the notes, at his hands lying on the desk, and saw the scar.

Deliberately, enduring the pain, he dragged his mind back. Heat, noise, clouds of choking dust clogging his pores and making it difficult to breathe, and the screams. Always the screams.

Desire drained away, as he had known it would, leaving him empty and shaken.

He stood up and went out of the office to the staff-room, pouring himself a cup of coffee with hands that were not quite steady.

'Hi. Any left?'

The voice behind him was soft, and his breath jammed in his throat again. He let it out consciously.

'Just about enough,' he said, and his voice sounded harsh, scrapy.

He was conscious of her eyes on him, mellow with concern. 'Are you OK?'

'Yes, I'm fine. Just a bit preoccupied.'

It was clearly a dismissal, and he felt a kick of self-disgust as rejection flickered over her gentle face and she withdrew into herself.

He made himself smile. 'Sorry. Clive Ronson. He was a bit of a mess. I was just writing up the notes.'

'Nick will sort him out if anyone can.'

She sounded very confident.

He felt he ought to warn her, just in case the worst happened. Ridiculous. She was a professional. If the man died, she would take it in her stride. Even so. . . 'He's bad,' Patrick warned. 'It'll be a few days before he's out of the woods, you know.'

'I know, but Nick's good,' she replied. 'Too good for the likes of Mr James and his private ankle. Pompous idiot. I gather he's still on the phone.'

Patrick felt the tension ease as they shared a smile. He noticed again how thin she was, how fine-drawn the skin over her delicate jawline.

'How about lunch?' he suggested into the ensuing silence.

'Lunch?' She said the word as if she had forgotten what it meant. He reminded her, and she laughed. 'I know what lunch is, silly. I just didn't realise it was time yet.'

He snorted softly. 'It's nearly one.'

'Oh. Right.'

'Shall I go and find a few sandwiches again?'

'That really isn't necessary——'

'What did you have for lunch yesterday?'

She shook her head. 'Nothing. I was too busy.'

'And Tuesday?'

She sighed, recognising defeat when it stared her in the face. 'Lunch would be lovely, but let me pay for it.'

He growled softly under his breath, and she suppressed a smile. 'I mean it.'

'Stubborn woman. All right, you can pay for your share. OK?'

She nodded.

Sensible woman. She knew when to give up, he thought with an inward chuckle.

He headed for the door, but as he got there a phone rang in the office.

Kathleen stuck her head out. 'That was ambulance control. A lorry's embedded in the front of a house, and the driver's trapped. He's still alive, but he's bad, and it'll be hours before they can get him out. They want a team.'

Anna joined him at the door. 'Do you want us to go?' she asked.

'Will you?'

She nodded. 'OK. Patrick?'

'Sure. Let me speak to them, find out what they know so we're prepared.'

He left Anna finding the emergency bag used for attending such accidents, and quickly established what else they would need.

His stomach rumbled, but he ignored it. He could eat later. Just now he had to get back on the merry-go-round.

Anna was appalled. The lorry was buried right inside the house, the cab almost invisible. As they arrived a fireman crawled out of a tiny hole near the left of the cab and shook his head.

'I can't really reach him. There just isn't enough room—oh, hi, Doc. Want to try and get through? He can talk, but not a lot else. I haven't got a glimpse of him yet.'

Anna took a breath. 'I could try and get closer. I'm smaller than you two.'

'Out of the question; it's too dangerous,' the fireman said bluntly.

'For who?' she asked him, her voice quiet. 'For you, for me, or for the driver?'

'He's right, Anna,' Patrick said slowly. 'That whole lot looks very unstable.'

'And what about the man inside it? How stable is he?'

The fireman shifted awkwardly. 'We don't know. He says his head's bleeding, and the steering-wheel's stuck in his abdomen, but we haven't been able to get anyone in there.'

'Well, you can now,' Anna said with quiet determination. She took his hat off his head, plonked it on her own and headed for the little gap. Taking a steadying breath, she squeezed into the hole and wriggled forward, feeling her way towards the front. She could see a heavy beam of some sort lying across the front of the cab, and the door had burst open, jamming across her path. The hat was in the way, so she took it off and dropped it behind her.

'Anna?'

Patrick's voice. 'I'm OK,' she called back.

Squeezing out her breath, she wriggled through the narrow gap and up into the side of the cab. Her right hand went into a pool of something sticky, and she sniffed. Blood. Lots of it.

'Hi, there,' she said, squeezing as much reassurance as possible into her voice.

A grunt of pain came out of the dim cab, and she ducked her head beneath the beam that was lying above her head and peered up towards his face. Blood was oozing steadily down his cheek from a wound high up on his temple. His eyes were bright, though, and alert. That was a good sign.

'What's your name?' she asked, knowing that it might be vital in ensuring his co-operation later in the rescue.

'Nigel—Nigel Ward.'

'OK, Nigel, let's find out how you are. Where do you hurt?'

'Everywhere. Head, chest, legs—especially my right leg.'

She was relieved about that. 'Hang on to the pain,' she told him. 'As long as you can feel, you're alive.'

He grinned, a surprising flash of white in the dark cab. 'I'll bear it in mind.' His voice was wry and filled with pain. She reached out and touched his hand, offering comfort.

'I'm Anna,' she told him. 'I'm a nurse at the hospital. There's a doctor outside but he's too big to get in here at the moment. I just want to find out how you're doing, and then they can start making plans to get you out. I'm going to have to go again, to get some equipment. I need to take some blood so we can cross-match and replace what you've lost, and I'll need to measure your blood pressure and bring you some pain relief, and maybe some supports for this beam before they can start shifting things. OK?'

'Will you be long?' he asked, and she felt rather than heard the fear in his voice.

'No,' she said firmly. 'Just a minute or two. I'll talk to you as I go, and I can talk to you from outside as well——'

'Anna?'

Patrick's voice was muffled but audible.

'See?' she told Nigel. 'You can hear people outside. OK, Patrick,' she called towards the door. 'I'm coming out. I need to do his BP, and I'll need an IV set and

Haemacel, a syringe for bloods, Entonox and some bandages—oh, and saline for cleaning a head-wound. I'm coming out.'

She squeezed Nigel's hand, glad to feel the pressure returned, and then wriggled out backwards. She was beginning to feel like a worm stuck in a tunnel.

Her dress caught on a sharp bit of metal jutting out and she heard it tear.

Still, she was free. She squirmed slowly backwards, and then there were hands on her waist and she was being pulled out and up into the fresh air.

'OK?'

It was Patrick, his face concerned, his voice gruff and scratchy.

She nodded, relieved to be out in the sunlight. 'He's alive, but his right arm's gone—it's lying at a funny angle. His back hurts, and his legs.'

'Thank God for that. At least he can still feel them.'

'That's what I thought. He's got a head-wound, and the steering-wheel's rammed firmly in under his ribs. I can just about see his face, but there's a beam lying right in front of it across the top of the cab.'

'Could I get in to him?'

She shook her head. 'Not a chance. If we'd had lunch I don't think I'd get in either.'

His face was grim. 'You'll have to do it all yourself, then.'

'Mmm. Can I have all the stuff? The first thing I want to do is take some blood for cross-matching. I can get to his left arm, so I should be able to get a line in and then we can start transfusing him. I want to keep a close eye on his BP, as well. He's got the steering-wheel in his abdomen and that's going to mess up his venous return, I expect. I think the wheel's intact. If it's broken, and penetrated through the wall, he's in much more serious trouble.'

Patrick nodded, assembling the things she'd requested while she stuck her head back in the hole and talked to Nigel for a moment.

'How is he?' Patrick asked.

'Still talking. I don't want to mess about, though. I wonder what's the best way to get that stuff in there?'

'I'll crawl in behind you as far as I can and pass things through to you, OK?' Patrick suggested. 'You can hand me back the syringe and I'll deal with the bottles. A police car can take the blood to haematology for cross-matching. Then I can be on hand to tell you what to do.'

'Just what I need, a bossy-boots up my tail,' she quipped, but she was reassured to know he was going to be there, just in case.

She took a steadying breath and crawled back into the hole, then, with Patrick behind her, she squirmed back into the cab.

'Hello, Nigel, I'm back,' she told him. 'How are things?'

'Better now you're here again,' he said quietly. She could feel the fear again, and squeezed his hand.

'There's a doctor behind me. He can't get in, but he can pass me things and we can talk to him. OK?'

'OK.'

His voice was getting weaker, she thought, and, turning with difficulty, she asked for the IV set.

Patrick reached up to her, the packaged set already in his hand.

There was an elastic strap in her pocket—when was she ever without one?—and she pulled it tight around Nigel's upper arm and turned his arm over carefully. The vein on the back of his forearm just above his wrist looked good, considering the amount of blood he had probably lost, and she prepared the site with an alcohol swab, wiping away the brick-dust and sweat that had clogged on the skin.

'OK, I'm going to put this into your arm now, Nigel. You'll just feel a little scratch coming up now. . .'

It was incredibly awkward doing it with her left hand, but she couldn't turn either of them round enough to do it with her right. Still, the needle slipped home on the first try and she heaved a quiet sigh of relief as she taped the tubes in place on his arm and plugged the syringe into the end.

Having filled it, she passed it back to Patrick and then held out her hand for the Haemacel.

He put it in her hand, his fingers warm and hard against hers, and she took comfort from the small contact.

The only place to hang the bag was from the rear-view mirror, but there it dangled right in her way so she had to dodge even further to see him.

She did so now, and managed a grim-lipped smile.

'OK?' she checked.

'I'll do.'

She slipped the blood pressure cuff on to his arm and checked his pressure. Low, as she had known it would be. Hopefully he wouldn't understand the significance of the numbers when she told Patrick. She opened up the drip so it ran in steadily.

'I'm just going to report to the doctor so he doesn't feel totally redundant,' she said with a smile, and then, squirming round, she bent over and stuck her head out of the gap.

'BP 90 over 40,' she told him quietly.

He swore under his breath. 'Internal?'

She shrugged. 'We need to get him out, Patrick, but there's this big beam over the cab, and if you tried to pull it out it would crush him. God knows what's holding it up as it is.'

His jaw muscle jerked, his mouth a harsh line. 'Are you sure I couldn't fit?'

She snorted softly. 'Don't be crazy. There's hardly room for me in here. You'll just have to tell me what to do.'

'Get out. I want to come in there.'

'No. You're being absurd. You'll just have to trust me.'

'It isn't a case of trust,' he muttered. 'You shouldn't be in there. It's no place for a woman——'

'Cut the heroism, Patrick,' she told him brusquely. 'Nigel doesn't have time for all that stuff.'

His mouth tightened, but he had no choice. 'Find out as much as you can about his condition,' he grunted. 'I'll get the Entonox.'

He backed out and went to confer with the firemen while she turned round and ducked back down to see her patient. She would have to deal with his head-wound, but she could see it had stopped bleeding now. She wiped it with cotton wool squeezed out in saline, and dabbed it dry, talking to him all the while. She had to find out as much as possible, and like this she could watch his eyes. 'Tell me more about your injuries,' she coaxed. 'Can you be specific about where you hurt?'

He thought for a moment. 'My right knee,' he said slowly. 'That's bloody sore. And my chest—right at the bottom. My stomach really.'

She turned her head and looked down at where the steering-wheel disappeared under the jut of his ribs. 'I'd like to feel it, see what I can find out about where that steering-wheel's pressing on you. Tell me if I hurt you,' she added, and then, slipping her fingers under the edge of his shirt, she ran her hand carefully over his ribs. Several were sticking out at a strange angle, but the skin seemed intact.

She worked her way down, her fingers tracing his

hipbone on the far side. So far so good. Her hand explored the rim of the steering-wheel, and she could feel something warm and wet on his abdomen. It didn't feel sticky, so it was probably urine. Certainly she could smell it. The question was, had his bladder been punctured or had he simply wet himself?

She asked, and he didn't seem to know. Still, there was no evidence of blood on her hand, which was a good sign. She continued her search, her fingers gentle but thorough, and found the full sweep of the steering-wheel, distorted but intact. So far, so good. She moved on.

His right femur seemed all right, lying awkwardly but unbroken, as far as she could tell. His knee, though, was a different matter. She approached it with caution, but the really painful part was embedded in the remains of the dashboard. The area below his knee was out of reach, but she could see in the light from the torch Patrick had passed her that it was trapped in the distorted footwell.

His left leg seemed to have fared better, and he said he could wriggle the toes of that one although she couldn't see them because of the bent and twisted metal in the way.

His voice was growing weaker, and she checked his blood pressure again. It was falling still, but whether because he was losing blood internally or because the steering-wheel was digging into his abdomen so hard it interferred with his venous flow she couldn't tell.

She squeezed the bag of Haemacel for a minute, to boost his circulation, and then turned her attention back to Patrick, who was calling her from the tunnel.

'They want to know about this beam. They're going to send in the smallest man they've got to check it out and put in supports and airbags, if necessary, to protect him while they remove the rubble from around the cab. OK? So you have to come out.'

Just then she sensed rather than heard a change in Nigel. 'Hang on,' she muttered, and, turning, she wriggled back towards him. 'Nigel?'

'It's getting bloody hard to breathe,' he muttered.

She flashed the torch at his face, noting the blue line round his lips and the bulging veins in the side of his neck.

'I'm just going to check your ribs,' she told him, and tapped the side of his chest nearest to her.

Sure enough, it sounded hollow and unduly loud.

She wriggled back to Patrick. 'I don't like to rock the boat,' she said quietly, 'but our patient's got a tension pneumothorax—I think his right lung's collapsed.'

Patrick's language deteriorated rapidly. 'You'll have to come out and let me in.'

'Don't be ridiculous. Get me a cannula and I'll do it.'

'With or without anaesthetic?'

'We don't have time to wait for the lignocaine to work. Just give me the stuff and talk me through it. If it hurts, no doubt he'll be grateful later.'

Muttering, clearly reluctant, he handed her the cannula. 'Between the fourth and fifth ribs, to the side and just below his nipple. And for God's sake mind the intercostal nerve and blood vessels—they run just below each rib.'

'Fine. Got that.' Cutting away Nigel's shirt, she cleaned the area quickly and opened the packet containing the cannula.

'Right, Nigel, I'm going to make a hole through into your ribcage and let out the air that's trapped outside your lung stopping you from breathing—OK? I'm sorry, it may hurt a bit.'

Nigel, now desperate for air, nodded. She guessed the other side of his chest might have similar problems, or perhaps a haemothorax. Whatever, if she didn't move soon, he was going to die.

Taking a steadying breath, and with Patrick's calm voice instructing her from behind, she slid the thick, solid trocar instrument through the intercostal muscle, which filled the space between the ribs, and into the pleural cavity, then slid the cannula over it and withdrew the trocar. There was a rush of air, and within seconds Nigel's colour changed back to a healthier pink.

'Better?' she asked, attaching a non-return valve to the line and taping it to his side.

'Hurts like hell,' he told her, but his eyes were brighter and he managed a grin. 'Thanks, Anna.'

She returned the grin. 'My pleasure. Right, let's get you out of here.'

CHAPTER THREE

PATRICK felt sick.

The dust, the noise, the rubble—the horror of that day two years ago came pouring back over him in a tidal wave of terror. The only things missing were the screams of the victims and the sobbing and wailing of their relatives.

Lying wedged beside the mangled cab, passing equipment up to Anna, the agonising memory of that day threatened to paralyse him. Only Anna's voice, calm and sensible, even managing to joke from time to time, kept him sane. That and having a job to do.

Being unable to get to the patient to do his job didn't help, either.

The business of the tension pneumothorax was horrendous. Anna was so calm, so unflappable, so brave about performing a fairly tricky medical procedure under such appalling conditions. He had handed her the equipment, taking strength from the touch of her hand, hopefully giving her strength too with the touch of his.

Never had contact seemed so important.

At last she gave him the all-clear and announced that Nigel was stable and the air was clearing from his pleural cavity. Relief made him feel weak.

'Right,' he called to her. 'We're going to start shifting stuff off the top now. Keep away from the windscreen if you can, and protect Nigel if possible. OK?'

'OK,' she replied, her voice muffled but calm. Damn, she must be exhausted.

Squirming backwards out of the hole, he climbed up

on top of the cab and helped shift the loose rubble. Once they could see the beam, it was clear that the heavy lifting gear brought in would have to be used to raise it before the lorry could be pulled clear.

And the cab would need support. Already it was sagging dangerously, and at one point the beam shifted and the cab roof groaned ominously.

Anna was still in there, risking her damn-fool neck to save a man she didn't know—doing exactly what he himself would have done if only he'd been small enough.

They paused to allow the heavy lifting gear to manoeuvre into position. Anna came out and the skinny little fireman tried again to wriggle into the cab with a hydraulic jack to support the roof.

Even he was too big, so in desperation they sent Anna in again, and passed up the heavy jacks into the cab, where she had to do the job of the fireman.

She went back into the hell-hole, a little grim-faced but quite calm. Patrick wanted to stop her, but there seemed little point in making a scene. Her contribution was the only one so far that had made any material difference to their patient. He could hardly ignore that and strong-arm her out of the way.

Finally, the jacks were secured to her satisfaction, and the lifting gear creaked and groaned and dragged the beam up and out of the way.

More rubble cascaded on to the roof of the cab, bringing a scream of pain from Nigel as one heavy block smashed through the remains of the windscreen on to his broken right arm.

As the rubble settled Patrick could hear Anna soothing Nigel, her voice calm and gentle, encouraging him.

'You're doing really well. Just hang on. You'll be out in a minute. They've got the cab clear now, so they can tow you out.'

Patrick heard a mumbled reply, and then Anna laughed.

'I'm flattered,' she said, her voice rich with something age-old and feminine that made Patrick's gut twist with jealously.

Damn, the man was chatting her up! He banged on the roof.

'How's it going down there?'

'OK. How long now?'

'Just a couple of minutes. They're shoring up the front of the house and then they're going to pull the lorry out. You'd better come out, Anna.'

There was silence for a minute, then her voice drifted out to him. 'Sorry, can't. The doorway's bunged up with rubble. I'll be OK in here. Just go ahead.'

Patrick didn't like it, but they really had no choice, and they couldn't justify wasting time freeing Anna first before pulling the cab out. Nigel had already been trapped for over four hours, and there was a very real danger of renal failure due to crush syndrome if he stayed there much longer.

'OK, let's roll,' the fire officer in charge called, and seconds later the area was cleared and the lorry was towed backwards out of the remains of the house. They only moved it far enough for safety, then Patrick was there, yanking open the passenger door and all but dragging Anna out into his arms.

He hugged her hard, said, 'Well done. Brave girl,' and then dived into the space she had vacated. 'Nigel? I'm Patrick Haddon, the doctor. How are you doing?'

Nigel looked at him and grinned weakly. 'You're not as pretty as Anna,' he slurred, and then his eyes drifted shut and he passed out.

'OK, let's get this cab opened up,' the fire officer was saying. He peered in through the driver's window at Patrick. 'How is he?'

'Not good. He's out at the moment. This steering-wheel is putting huge pressure on his abdomen, but I don't want it moved until the very last second, because once we take it out his circulation will collapse. Can you free his legs first, and perhaps take off the roof and sides so we can get at him better?'

It took another half-hour, during which the only analgesia they could give Nigel was the Entonox gas, because when they had given him a little pethidine earlier it had crashed his blood pressure and it was already dangerously low. They couldn't risk a repeat at this stage.

The Entonox was better than nothing but not much, and Patrick gripped Nigel's good hand hard while they eased the dashboard away from his shattered knee. Mercifully he passed out, and they worked quickly to remove the rest of the footwell from around his legs. Finally the only thing holding Nigel in place was the steering-wheel. The ambulancemen managed to get a spinal splint on, supporting the upper part of his back and his neck, but they were unable to splint the lower part because of the pressure from the steering-wheel. They would splint all of it again when he was released.

Anna was on one side of him, supporting his arm which was now protected by an inflatable splint, and Patrick was on the other, squeezing the bag of whole blood into him as hard as he dared. The cross-matched supplies had arrived some time ago and had been steadily dripping into him, but now, in preparation for the circulatory collapse Patrick felt was imminent, he wanted him topped right up.

'OK,' he said when he was ready, and Anna held the Entonox mask and told the now-conscious Nigel to breathe the gas while they removed the steering-column.

At the first push of the hydraulic jack Nigel

screamed, a sound that brought bile to Patrick's throat, and he gripped his hand while Anna turned the valve on the Entonox so that the supply of painkilling gas flowed steadily over his face without requiring any effort or control of the mask.

'You're doing well,' Patrick told him. 'Just hang on.'

'I can't,' he groaned.

'Yes, you can,' Anna said calmly. 'You're nearly out, Nigel. Hang on in there.'

At a nod from Patrick the fireman continued, the pneumatic jack creaking as the steering-column was pushed steadily out of the way. As soon as it was free the ambulancemen moved in, sliding the full spinal support into position and strapping it round Nigel before lifting the now unconscious man out of the cab and on to the waiting stretcher.

Moments later it was ready to go.

'I'll go with him,' Patrick said. 'Can you drive?'

Anna nodded, and he threw her the keys of his car.

'It's insured for any driver, but take care. I'll see you back at the hospital.'

Without giving his father's extremely costly Jaguar another thought, Patrick bounded into the back of the ambulance and the doors slammed behind him.

Anna stared at the keys in her hand, then at the car, sleek, low and very expensive-looking. She felt shaken and battered, her body cramped from hours in the cab, her nerves strung to breaking-point.

During one of the fireman's attempts to get in the cab she had rung her childminder and asked if she would have Flissy for the night. It was obvious that they weren't about to get away quickly, and it wouldn't have occurred to her to do anything but stay.

So there was no small, warm body at home waiting

for a hug; no one, in fact, to care that she had just spent one of the most traumatic afternoons of her life.

Numbly she let herself into Patrick's car and started the engine, wondering idly how a mere SR could afford a beast of that ilk. The engine was so quiet she thought for a moment it hadn't started, but then she heard the low grumble of the exhaust and nodded.

Now, the gears.

Ah.

Another surprise. It was an automatic. She had never driven an automatic, but working on the principle that it was simply one less pedal to push, she pulled the lever back to D.

The car jerked forward, and she stamped her foot on the brake and sighed.

A friendly face appeared at the window. 'Having trouble, love?'

She looked up at Ron Hargreaves, the policeman who had been on hand all afternoon, and switched off the engine. 'You could say that. Patrick wants me to drive his car back to the hospital but I've never driven an automatic.'

'Are you insured?' he asked immediately.

'Patrick said so. He said it was insured for any driver.'

'Then I'll drive you back. You look done in. Bert can follow in the squad car and drive me back from the hospital. OK?'

She nodded, relief flooding through her. It wasn't that she minded trying it, but it had been a particularly difficult day and she just didn't feel up to the task.

She slid over to the passenger side, bumping her hip on the handbrake, and after a brief exchange with the other policeman Ron slid in beside her and started the engine again. 'Always fancied driving one of these,' Ron confessed, and, pulling smoothly out into the traffic, he followed the road through the town centre to the hospital.

Arriving at the entrance to A and E, he parked the car where she showed him and they both got out.

'Thank you, Ron,' Anna said with feeling. 'I would have hated to wrap it round a tree!'

Ron laughed. 'Pleasure. Like I said, I've often fancied a drive in one. I'll come in with you and see how Nigel's doing,' he suggested, and Anna went with him, her tiredness forgotten again.

Patrick was standing in the office with Jack Lawrence, his face weary.

'How's Nigel?' she asked.

'Lousy. He's gone up to Theatre—his circulation all but collapsed when the pressure was released. We nearly lost him in the ambulance. Ross Hamilton's opening him up to check for a ruptured spleen and bowel, while Nick Davidson does the arm and the knee.'

Anna nodded. Ross was one of the surgical consultants and very skilled.

'What about his head-wound?' she asked.

'Superficial. Did you get here OK?'

'Ron drove me back,' she told him. 'I didn't fancy tearing the side out of your car.'

A fleeting smile touched his lips, but then he turned back to Jack. 'This is the real heroine of the afternoon, of course,' he said. 'We would have lost him hours ago without her.'

She blushed and demurred, but Ron agreed and she found herself outvoted.

'She looks bushed. Why don't you take her home?' Jack said quietly.

'Good idea,' Patrick agreed. 'Is your car here?'

She shook her head. 'It's off the road at the moment, waiting for a part.'

Or, more precisely, waiting for the money to pay for the part, but she didn't bother to elaborate. The idea of a lift home was suddenly immensely appealing, and she went and gathered up her things and trailed back to the entrance.

Patrick was waiting, in conversation with Ron, and as she walked up to them he turned and smiled and warmed her right down to her toes.

'All set?' he asked softly.

She nodded.

'Come on, then.' Resting his hand lightly in the small of her back, he ushered her out into the quiet of the evening. Settling her in the passenger seat, he went round and slid behind the wheel, then shot her a grin. 'Where to?'

'Mulberry Terrace—do you know it? It's off Spring Road.'

'Yes.'

How odd, she thought, if he's new to the area. But perhaps he wasn't. He'd found the way to the accident site without any prompting from her, although she hadn't given it a thought at the time.

'Are you local?' she asked now.

'I used to be. My parents live here still.'

She settled back against the leather upholstery, more than content with silence. She felt suddenly shattered, too tired to move, and the quiet comfort of the car lulled her almost to sleep.

They arrived at Mulberry Terrace all too soon, and she pointed out her tiny terraced house and gathered her things from around her feet while he slid the huge car neatly into a gap just inches bigger.

'Would you like a cup of coffee?' she asked.

Sheer good manners had prompted the suggestion, but in truth she was too tired to cope with the social niceties. So, fortunately, was Patrick.

'I'll just see you in, then I could do with going home and having a shower, and I expect you could do with a long, hot soak.'

The idea was sheer luxury.

She fumbled in her bag for the keys of the house, and he waited patiently until she had found them and slipped the key into the lock.

She thought he would go then, and turned to thank him, but he followed her over the step and shut the door.

'Changed your mind?' she asked.

He shook his head, and she was suddenly over-whelmingly aware of him in the narrow confines of the the little hall.

'I just wanted to thank you for what you did today,' he said softly. 'I meant what I said about courage. Getting into a confined space under tons of rubble takes real grit. I know that—I've done it—and I know just what that fear feels like. I just wanted to thank you, for Nigel.'

Ridiculous tears prickled behind her eyelids and she blinked hard. 'Anyone would have done it.'

'Not anyone.'

'Anyone there today.'

'That's different, but it still doesn't make it any easier to have done it.'

He drew her gently into his arms, cradling her head against the hard expanse of his chest.

He smelled of sweat and dust and diesel, but it was the most potent and heady aphrodisiac Anna could imagine. Her arms slid round his waist, and her head tipped back to receive the kiss she had been waiting for all week.

When it came it was tentative, a gentle exploration of her mouth by his warm, firm lips. They sipped and brushed, and then finally with a muttered groan they settled against hers and claimed them.

She clung to him, her legs suddenly weak, her body yearning for the strength and support of his. Yearning, too, for something else, something she had never known but only this week had dreamed of.

She felt the hot, slick velvet of his tongue trace her lips and she opened to him, a sharp stab of desire piercing her as he searched the deep and secret recesses of her mouth.

Her fingers found his hair, threading among the rich strands, pulling him down harder against her mouth with a soft cry of need as she arched against him, seeking the masculine counterpoint to the womanhood raging within her. She felt him stiffen, then his hand slid down her spine and eased her up against him, leaving her in no doubt about his commitment to the kiss.

He was with her all the way. Her own tongue grew bold, seeking his out and dallying with it in a dance as old as time. A ragged groan rose in his throat and for an instant he gave in to the savage need that claimed them.

Then his hands gripped her shoulders, and gently but firmly eased her away from him.

'No,' he said, his voice roughened but implacable. 'Not like this, not when you're so tired you hardly know what you're doing.'

Common sense and shame washed over her in equal measure. Dear God, what was she doing, coming on to him like that? And he was married! Oh, what was she doing?

She stepped back, almost stumbling over the edge of the mat, and he reached out and steadied her.

'I'm sorry,' she mumbled, her pride in tatters. 'Whatever must you think of me, doing that? Oh, Lord——'

'Don't.' His hand tipped her chin, and she forced herself to look at him. Stunned, she absorbed the desire raging in his eyes, the tiredness, the lines of strain around his mouth—and the rueful regret. 'You're overtired, scared and elated all at once. What you really need is a hot bath and an early night, not me climbing all over you like a randy adolescent.'

The self-disgust in his voice made her blink. He really thought it was his fault? Apparently. Although who was climbing all over whom was a moot point. With one last, blisteringly tender brush of his lips over hers he was gone, leaving her standing in the hall in a welter of emotions.

Not least was confusion.

She got up early in the morning and went to her childminder, to have breakfast with her daughter and to see her before the start of the day.

It wasn't the first time this sort of thing had happened, and doubtless it wouldn't be the last, but she liked to make the start of Flissy's day as ordinary as possible and so she took her to playgroup on her way to the hospital.

Of course she still didn't have her car and so she was late, rushing in hot and bothered at five past nine.

'You're here!' Kathleen said, in surprise as she passed the office door.

'Of course I'm here—I'm on duty nine till five, Monday to Friday, remember?'

Kathleen laughed softly. 'Well, so you are. Fancy me forgetting a silly thing like that.'

'Cut the sarcasm,' Anna said tiredly. 'I feel shattered.'

'So you do, I expect. That's why I'm surprised you're here. I heard what you did. Well done.'

Anna waved her comments aside, embarrassed all

over again. 'Don't tell me this is going to go on all day,' she groaned.

Kathleen chuckled. 'Sorry. No more sycophancy. But if you want to go home early, that's fine.'

She hung up her coat and pinned on her hat, then went back to Kathleen's office. 'Kath, is Patrick around today?' she asked, as casually as possible.

'Sure—he's been here since eight. He's in the plaster-room at the moment, checking out a swollen limb. Go on in.'

'Oh, no,' she said, backing out of the office. 'I just wondered if there was any news on the lorry driver.... Shall I go and do a bit of Triage? It looks rather full out there.'

'Good idea. I'm just scribbling up these notes and I'll be with you.'

Anna went and picked up the pile of waiting notes, scanned through them and then picked the patients out in rough order of priority.

The most urgent case, a child with a partially severed finger, went straight in with Kath seconds later.

Another child, this one with a query fractured radius, went next on her list, followed by a man with a cut over his eyebrow that was bleeding very freely despite all attempts to stop it. They were both priority two.

A man with a badly wrenched thumb and torn nail was given priority three, and told to expect a wait of around half an hour. He argued that he had been there longer than the child who had already gone in, and the other two patients she had just seen.

Anna explained the priority system to him, and he glared at her. 'I'm in agony, girl! I should be a priority two at least!'

Anna sighed inwardly. 'I'm sorry, the other cases in front of you were in more urgent need of attention——'

'In whose opinion?' he bristled.

She hung on to her temper with difficulty. 'In mine,' she replied, her voice implacable, and showed him back out to the waiting-area.

'I'll report you,' he threatened.

'Feel free,' she said, beyond caring.

The office phone rang and she answered it in Kath's absence, then went and found her.

'Motorcyclist coming in—back, leg and head injuries.'

Kathleen's mouth tightened. Despite her pleas, Jack still had his motorbike, and although she knew he was careful, it was still a risk. Anna knew how she must feel, and shot her a sympathetic smile.

'Get Jack to deal with it,' Kathleen said briskly now. 'Perhaps it'll give the mad fool something to think about.'

Anna smiled again and went to prepare Crash and alert X-ray, Neurosurgery, Orthopaedics and Theatre. She found Jack topping up the coffee-machine, and he went with her to wait at the door.

A few moments later the ambulance arrived, going very slowly, and they unloaded the young man with great care.

To Anna's surprise he was conscious, but there was blood seeping down the back of his helmet.

'Head hurts,' he was mumbling, tugging at the helmet feebly.

Jack removed his hands from the helmet. 'Leave the helmet for now. I want your head X-rayed before we move it, and your spine. Just lie there. We'll get you comfortable as soon as possible.'

Anna took charge of the IV bag running Haemacel into his arm, and very carefully, so as not to jog the trolley, they wheeled him through into Crash and cut away his tattered leathers. His left femur, or thigh bone, was clearly snapped clean in half, and his foot lay at a strange angle.

'That ankle's gone, too. I'll spring his ribs and pelvis and check the rest.'

Very carefully, watching the boy's face all the time, Jack quickly checked his whole body for damage, dictating a veritable catalogue of injuries to Anna, including several broken ribs, known as a Flail chest, possible ruptured spleen, and multiple abrasions in addition to his left leg and the head injuries that they couldn't begin to assess.

'I want whole body X-rays, but particularly his head and spine. And for God's sake leave that helmet on.'

They wheeled him through to X-ray, and after all the shots were taken Jack stood and stared at the screen in horror.

His skull was fractured despite the helmet, but, perhaps more critically, he had an undisplaced fracture of the second cervical vertebra.

'It's a good job nobody yanked his helmet off,' Anna murmured.

'Too right,' Jack said softly, and went back to him.

'Right, my friend, I want you to keep very, very still for me. You've got several very nasty fractures, and I want you immobilised before we take you anywhere— OK?'

The boy stared at him blankly, then his lips moved.

'Hurt,' he murmured.

Jack turned to Anna. 'Where the hell is the neuro-surgeon? His right pupil's fixed and dilated. I suspect he's got compression from a bleed somewhere in there. Let's face it, it would be a miracle if he hadn't. Do a coma score on him for me, could you, while I ring Neurosurgery and bully them?'

He left her with their patient, and moments later her spine prickled and a soft voice sounded by her ear.

'Hi.'

Her heart lurched. What a time to meet, after that blistering kiss of the night before. She closed her eyes, hoping it was a dream, but when she opened them he was still there. 'Morning,' she mumbled indistinctly, giving her patient all her attention. Lord, he looked grim, poor lad. Patrick looked down at him and winced.

'Ouch.'

'Quite. I'm trying to do a Glasgow coma score, but he keeps going down as I do it. I think I'd better call Jack now.'

Jack appeared then anyway, took one look at the patient and sighed.

'They're on their way. Theatre's alerted already, but I have a sneaking feeling they're wasting their time.'

As they watched, the monitor Anna had set up bleeped and settled into a straight line.

Jack swore.

'Are we going to do anything?' Patrick asked.

Jack looked at him, and then up at the X-rays—the skull fractured like an eggshell and yet still virtually intact, the neck injury precluding any attempt to intubate him.

'We can try,' he said, without much hope.

Anna bagged the patient, the mask held firmly over his face through the visor of his helmet, while Patrick worked with Jack on his chest, injecting atropine, adrenaline, calcium—and a shot of adrenaline directly into his heart.

Nothing. Not a flicker.

They worked on him for nearly half an hour, through the arrival of the neurosurgeon, the orthopaedic surgeon and the anaesthetist.

Finally Jack swore again, washed his hands, and

hurled the paper towel across the room, glaring at the dead boy.

'What a bloody waste,' he growled.

Kathleen stuck her head round the door. 'His mum's here—how is he?'

'Dead,' Jack said flatly. 'He's dead. Where is she?'

Kathleen's face drained of colour. 'In the interview room.'

'OK, I'll see her. Get him ready for her to see, could you?' he said to Anna.

'What about the helmet?'

He snorted. 'Take it off. It can't do any harm any more, can it?' He took a steadying breath, closed his eyes for a moment, and then went out into the corridor.

Anna turned back to Patrick, and together they took the helmet off, then wiped the worst of the blood from the boy's lifeless face and covered his broken body with a blanket.

The other medical staff left the room, their presence no longer required, and, after checking that he was ready for his mother to see, Anna stayed while the shocked and grief-stricken woman came in, stared in silence at her son and then left, clearly numb.

The pain, Anna knew, would come later. Covering the body again, she followed Kathleen, who was looking devastated. She found her in the staff-room, curled up on a chair, her eyes staring.

'Kath?' she said softly.

Kathleen turned towards her, her eyes filled with pain. 'Why does he insist on riding it? That could have been him, Anna, but he just won't give up. He promised, but he just won't give up, and now——'

Anna waited, but she didn't go on, instead finding a tissue and blowing her nose hard. 'Sorry. I'm a mess.'

'You are. You're not usually this bad. I mean, I know you don't like losing patients, none of us do, but you're taking it so personally.' She took Kathleen's hand. 'What's really wrong, Kath? Tell me.'

Her eyes were bleak. 'I'm pregnant, Anna,' she said softly, 'with a baby Jack doesn't want, and I don't know how to tell him.'

CHAPTER FOUR

ANNA was stunned.

'Pregnant?' she exclaimed softly. 'But—I thought——Oh, God, Kath, you haven't been having an affair?'

Kathleen laughed, the sound brittle to Anna's ears.

'No, of course not, but that's exactly what Jack's going to think, isn't it? How the hell do I persuade a man who had a vasectomy more than fifteen years ago that it just suddenly failed?'

Anna opened her mouth to comment, and closed it again without saying anything. There didn't seem to be anything sensible *to* say. And getting Jack to believe that the baby was his was only the start of the problems facing Kathleen.

'What are you going to do?' she asked gently.

'What can I do? I'll have it.'

'But what about the cystic fibrosis risk?'

'What about it?' Kathleen asked heavily. 'I'm pregnant, Anna. You of all people know what that means. Whatever might be wrong with my baby, it's *my* baby, and there's no way on God's earth I'll have an abortion just to satisfy Jack's paranoia.'

Anna sighed. Jack had had his vasectomy when his son had been diagnosed as having cystic fibrosis. He had lost Johnnie at the age of thirteen, but Kathleen had married him knowing he would never have another child.

Till now. Never was not, apparently, as far away as Jack had thought. She wondered how he would take it, but first of all he had to be persuaded that the child was his.

Anna didn't envy Kath one bit.

'How far on are you?' she asked now.

'Ten weeks. I did the test when I missed my second period.'

'And Jack hasn't noticed?'

Kath laughed. 'Don't sound so incredulous. He was away on a course for a few days a month ago. I suppose he's just lost track of the time. He'll realise soon, though, because I can't face filling up the coffee-machine and I was sick last night.'

Anna knew all about morning sickness. Most particularly she knew that the name was misleading, and that it could occur at any time of the day or night.

'Did Jack know?'

Kathleen shook her head. 'No. He was still here. He sent me on ahead because he wanted to be here when the lorry driver came in. How is he, by the way?'

'I don't know; I must find out. Kath, can I get you something? A cup of tea or a cold drink?'

The sister's smile was wan, but she shook her head. 'No, I'm fine. Thanks for offering. I'll go and deal with that poor boy's mother. Perhaps it'll take my mind off telling Jack.'

'Telling Jack what?'

Kath's face paled at the sound of her husband's voice.

Anna, not wishing to be in the midst of a marital confrontation about something so shatteringly important, excused herself and left the room, pulling the door to gently behind her.

She went to the interview room instead of Kath, to see the dead boy's mother, and discovered she had gone down to the chapel. She went out to the waiting-area, but there were no patients for a change.

'An unexpected bonus, especially after such a nasty

start,' Patrick said from behind her. 'I imagine it'll hot up later today, though, being Friday.'

'No doubt,' she replied drily, and cast about for something to say that wasn't directly connected with standing in his arms the night before, separated only by an inadequate layer of clothes that hid little from the imagination. One obvious topic sprang to mind, and she latched on to it with enormous enthusiasm. 'How's Nigel? Have you had time to find out yet?'

'No. I'll ring the ward now, if you like.'

'I would. I spent a lot of time with him yesterday. We got quite close.'

Patrick snorted softly. 'You don't say. He was chatting you up at one point.'

She chuckled. 'When the rubble fell in and I told him to hang on? He said if he hadn't already been married he'd make me an offer, I was better than Valium.'

Patrick laughed, the tension easing visibly from him, and she realised with a start that he had been jealous.

'Valium, eh? He obviously doesn't see you the way I do. The last thing I'd describe you as is a tranquilliser!'

Anna blushed. 'Perhaps you need a smashed knee to settle you down a little.'

'Ouch,' he said, and chuckled. 'Is that a threat?'

'I'm not sure,' she said bluntly. 'Let's go and find out how he is.'

They went together to the office and contacted ITU, to be told that he was doing so well he was expected to be transferred to Orthopaedics the following day. His knee was shattered, his ribs a mess and his pelvis had been very badly bruised, but otherwise he was fine, making excellent progress, and hadn't sustained any serious internal injuries.

'There we are. You saved his life, you clever girl.'

'Oh, Patrick, give it a rest,' she said with a blushing laugh, and he hugged her briefly as he stood up.

'Come on, it's lunchtime—well, almost. Today I'm taking you to lunch——'

'Patrick?'

Jack's voice sounded like a whipcrack, and Patrick broke off and turned towards the door, his eyebrows rising slightly in surprise at the shortness of his boss's tone.

'Yes?'

'Can you mind the shop? Kathleen and I are going for a walk somewhere quiet. We'll be back later.'

'Of course.'

They watched Jack go, his face like a thundercloud, and Kathleen resigned but unhappy behind him. He paused, taking her arm in a less than tender grip, and hustled her out.

'What the hell's eating them?' he asked softly.

Anna shook her head. 'I think it's best not to ask. It's rather sensitive.'

'Sensitive? Are you sure he won't kill her, whatever she's done?'

Anna's chin came up. 'She hasn't done anything. And I doubt if he'll kill her.'

Patrick's eyebrow arched at her tone. 'He did look very angry.'

'He is. He'll get over it.'

'Whatever it is.'

'As I said, it's private and very sensitive.'

'So butt out?'

'Exactly.'

'Fine.' He shrugged and folded his arms. 'So, once again we don't get lunch. How did I know this would happen?' he said with a sigh.

'There's coffee, and a tin of biscuits,' Anna reminded him.

He threw her a look of such disgust that she chuckled.

'You could always bribe Alvin to bring you something from the canteen the next time he passes it. He's just there.'

'Alvin?'

'The porter.'

Patrick's sorrowful brown eyes brightened and he headed for the door, following the ambling porter. 'Clever girl. Hey, Alvin!'

The man came back. 'Yes, Doc?'

Patrick stuck a ten-pound note in his hand. 'The next time you're passing the canteen, you couldn't stock us up with a few sandwiches, could you?'

His eyes flicked to Anna. 'Want some doughnuts, too, love? They've just made a batch.'

'You're a treasure. And, Alvin?'

He paused.

'Lots of tandoori chicken sandwiches.'

'Yes, ma'am. Certainly, ma'am. Anything else, ma'am?'

'Don't be cheeky—you might need me one day,' she told him, and he winked and ambled off, clearly as short of work as they were.

It didn't last, however. They were just sitting down to eat when Julie, the receptionist, popped her head round the door.

'Anna? Little visitor for you—got a cut on her hand. Can you come?'

She took another bite of her chicken sandwich, threatened Patrick with dire consequences if he pinched it, and followed the receptionist out.

A little girl was there, standing beside the reception desk with her childminder.

'Flissy!' Anna exclaimed.

'H'lo, Mummy. I hurt my hand.'

Anna crouched beside her little daughter, not in the least worried. Flissy looked too calm for anything drastic. Still, she deserved and would get her mother's undivided attention. 'What have you done, sweetheart?' she asked.

'I cut my hand at playgroup. I was helping Betty and I squashed up the playdough and there was a knife inside.'

'Oh, dear,' Anna said sympathetically, slowly unravelling the makeshift bandage round her daughter's hand. It wasn't the first time Flissy had been in to have some tiny injury kissed better by Mummy, and Anna was just glad that they were so quiet that lunchtime. She fully expected to find a tiny graze, but when she unfolded the little fingers it was to find quite a deep cut across the palm of her hand.

'Oh, darling!' she said, and hugged her, stifling her maternal panic. 'What a. . .splendid cut!'

Julie was hovering behind Flissy and caught Anna's eye.

'Patrick?' she mouthed, and Anna nodded. It would need stitching, and no doubt she would make the most awful fuss. One thing was sure, by the time he'd finished he'd be well aware that Flissy was her daughter. Oh, well. . .

She turned to her childminder. 'Sue, you are able to hang on? This shouldn't take too long, we're not busy at the moment, but we're a bit short-staffed so I can't leave early.'

'Sure,' Sue agreed. 'Just so long as I'm out in time to fetch my children from school.'

'Of course you will be. This won't take a minute, will it, Fliss?'

Flissy shook her head, setting her dark curls bobbing around her head, and Anna led her into a cubicle.

When Patrick came into the cubicle he found Anna

sitting on a chair with Flissy on her lap, one small hand cradled in the other, palm-up. He glanced at the cut as he walked in, and then looked up to meet Anna's eyes.

'That'll teach me to try and have lunch,' he said quietly with a grin, then dropped to his haunches and smiled gently at Flissy.

'Hello, sweetheart. What's your name?'

'Flissy—well, F'licity, really, but when I was tiny I couldn't say it so I called myself Flissy instead. I cut my hand.'

Patrick's mouth twitched. 'I see. May I look?' Her tiny hand disappeared inside his large one, resting trustingly in his palm as he studied the cut.

'How did you do it?'

Flissy told the story again, very impressed to have snagged a doctor this time, and Patrick kept his smile under control and gave the little girl his undivided attention.

'Well, Flissy,' he said thoughtfully, 'I'm afraid it's rather a big cut to heal all by itself, so we're going to give it a bit of help.'

'Does it need stitches?' she asked excitedly. 'Bobby had to have stitches when he cut his head—do you remember?'

She squirmed round and stared up at Anna, and Anna nodded. 'Yes, I do. And yes, it will need stitches.'

'Bobby had three.'

Patrick eyed the cut. 'In which case, young lady, I think you're going to beat him, because I think that rather wonderful cut of yours is going to need four, at least.'

Her eyes widened. 'Four? Oh, boy!'

Patrick's eyes, as he looked up at Anna, twinkled with amusement. Then he asked the question Anna had been dreading.

'Is Mum in the waiting-room?'

'Ah—not exactly.'

'Well, we need her here.'

'She's here,' Flissy said, clearly puzzled.

Not as puzzled as Patrick. 'Well, could we have her, then?' he said, slightly impatiently.

Anna sighed and forced herself to meet his eyes. 'I'm Flissy's mother,' she said quietly.

His jaw dropped, then he collected himself with commendable speed. 'Will you be all right doing this, or do you want someone else to help?'

'I'll be fine,' she assured him, although she wasn't convinced she would be. It all depended on Flissy.

Flissy, of course, was a star. Patrick warned her that the lignocaine would sting a bit, and she whimpered slightly and turned her head into Anna's chest, but her hand didn't move a fraction.

'Well done, Flissy,' Patrick said warmly as he withdrew the syringe. 'What a brave girl. I promise you, that really is the very worst bit. From now on what I have to do doesn't hurt at all,' he assured her.

She regarded him doubtfully through teary eyes. 'Promise?'

'I promise.'

His voice was so sincere that if he had promised Flissy the crown jewels, Anna would have expected him to produce them within minutes.

He prepared the trolley himself, cleaning up the wound and checking it thoroughly before he was ready to start. He gave the lignocaine plenty of time, but even so Anna didn't want to watch, and she was sure she didn't want Flissy to watch, either.

'Look, darling. Can you see that poster? What's on it?' she asked.

It was very much a spur-of-the-moment choice of distraction, and Anna regretted it instantly. The poster showed a woman breastfeeding her baby, and it led to a very interesting and searching discussion which was far too revealing for Anna's peace of mind, but since it kept Flissy's attention off her hand for the time being, Anna allowed it to run its course.

'There, all finished,' Patrick said, sitting back with an almost suppressed smile, and Anna was able to break off the difficult discussion and give her attention to the cut.

Flissy bent her head and inspected the neat row of sutures intently, then lifted her laughing face to Patrick. 'There are five!' she said proudly.

He grinned. 'I thought you ought to beat this Bobby properly, Flissy.'

He sprayed her hand with antiobiotic spray and then plastic skin, to cover the wound without the necessity of bandages, but he advised Anna to keep it covered with a light dry dressing for the first few days just to stop the stitches catching on things.

Then he straightened up and gave Anna a rather strained smile.

'Are you taking her home?'

She shook her head. 'No. She's going with Sue. I'll pick her up after work as usual.'

He opened his mouth to argue, but she glared at him and he shut it. 'Fine. Bye-bye, Flissy. I'll see you in a week to take those stitches out, OK?'

She nodded. 'Bye—and thanks for giving me five stitches. That's really cool.'

His grin was spontaneous and gentle. 'My pleasure.'

He disappeared through the curtain, and Anna let out the breath she had been holding almost since he walked in, she thought.

Of course she hadn't, but as she felt the tension drain she wondered what, exactly, she had been worried about.

His opinion of her, she acknowledged ruefully. When would she learn that the opinion of others was a luxury she couldn't afford? So long as she had her own pride—although after the way she had behaved with him last night she wasn't sure she should have any pride left at all. . .

'Can we show Sue?' Flissy was asking, and Anna slid her off her knee and led her back to the waiting-room. Hopefully there would be a queue of people waiting by now, and she could avoid the discussion she felt was coming.

Unfortunately she was out of luck. Handing Flissy over to Sue, she made her way back to the staff-room and her abandoned lunch, to find Patrick sitting there cradling a cup of coffee in his big hands.

He met her eyes, but his own were guarded, watchful.

'How is she?'

'Fine. I've handed her back to Sue.'

His mouth narrowed slightly, and she looked away, not prepared to get into a row with him about the upbringing of her child.

'It's a shame Kathleen isn't here to cover for you; you could have gone home with her. We should have enough cover for that sort of emergency.'

She laughed without humour. 'Funding,' she said shortly.

She helped herself to one of the doughnuts and a cup of coffee. Any minute now he'd ask about Flissy's father. Hell.

The doughnut was still slightly warm, and she bit into it, more careful this time with the jam. Still it dribbled a little, and she flicked out her tongue and chased the tiny dollop on her lip.

As she looked up and met his eyes over it, she

surprised a look of such naked desire that her breath caught.

Then it was gone, blanked out and replaced by a look of such contempt that she nearly dropped the doughnut.

'You should have told me you were married,' he said, his voice harsh. 'It never occurred to me, as you don't wear a ring. You should have said something, stopped me last night. I would never have kissed you if I'd realised you were married.'

'I started it,' she reminded him. 'And anyway, I'm not. I haven't got a husband.'

He made a dismissive noise. 'Partner, then.'

She shook her head. 'No—no husband, no partner, no nothing. Only Flissy. And you can talk! I may have started it, but you didn't exactly back out of that kiss. So don't get all moralistic about *my* personal life when you've got a wife of your own tucked up at home!'

His face blanched, the colour draining from his cheeks. For a long time he said nothing, then, as if he had to drag the words up from somewhere long-buried, he said, 'Isobel's dead.'

Anna felt her own colour drain.

'Oh, Lord, Patrick, I'm sorry,' she said, and then realisation dawned, breaking through the clouds in her mind with the subtlety of a searchlight. 'The earthquake?' she whispered.

His face was harsh, uncompromising, giving nothing away. 'Yes.'

It was all he said, but it explained so much—his reluctance to talk about the earthquake, the way he had reacted yesterday with the lorry buried in the rubble of the house, the almost savage way he had yanked her from the cab and dragged her into his arms, and, last but by no means least, the passionate intensity of the kiss.

It had meant nothing. She realised that now. It was just relief—relief that she was alive and all right, relief that the patient was still alive and stood a chance, and relief, too, that the nightmare was ended.

She looked down at her hands and realised they were trembling. It explained his reactions, but not her own. For her, the kiss had been exactly what it seemed—an affirmation of life, a need to hold him, to be close to him, to explore the new and frightening feelings that had haunted her sleep all week. She wanted him, and last night, for whatever reason, he had wanted her.

Now, however, that wanting was gone, banished by the pain she could see in his eyes.

She had discovered that he no longer had a wife, but instead of giving them an opportunity to be together, it merely kept them even further apart.

How could she possibly compete with a ghost?

Swallowing her coffee, she stood up and put the cup down, then paused, her hands rammed firmly in her pockets to stop her from running them through his hair and drawing his beloved face down to cradle him against her heart.

'I'll go and see if there's anyone out in the waiting-room,' she said, her voice catching slightly.

'Anna?'

She hesitated.

'About last night.'

'Yes?'

'I'm sorry. It was just circumstances that made me react like that. I hope I didn't give you the wrong idea.'

She controlled the little spurt of humourless laughter that rose in her chest. 'No. No, of course not. Excuse me.'

She went quietly up the corridor, her shoulders ramrod-straight, and almost pounced on the one woman sitting waiting.

She had a cut, a nasty jagged tear in one finger from a piece of barbed wire. Fortunately she wouldn't need Patrick to stitch it, because Anna had been trained in suturing and it was well within her capabilities.

Half an hour later the woman left, her finger neatly sewn up again, and Anna wondered how she could avoid Patrick for the rest of the afternoon.

Not that he was a threat. Oh, no. It was rather herself and her own reaction to him that was worrying her now. Never having been a victim of it before, she had taken her time recognising the symptoms of adolescent calf-love.

And twenty-six was a bit damned old to start, she thought in disgust. Oh, well, it could have been worse. At least he wasn't a raving sex-maniac and married, to boot.

She was in the office answering the phone when Kathleen marched in, tight-lipped and grimly silent.

Jack followed, no less grim-lipped but far from silent. 'I'm going down to the path lab now,' he gritted. 'There's no way that's my baby, and there's only one way to prove it. I'm going to settle this once and for all with a sperm-count—though how the hell they count something that doesn't exist we have yet to find out.'

And he turned on his heel and stalked off, head high, his usually laughing eyes snapping fire.

Kath sank down on to the edge of the desk, buried her face in her hands and burst into tears. Anna felt helpless. What could she say to comfort her friend in these circumstances? She finished the phone call, stood up and put her arms around Kath.

'Take it easy, Kath,' she murmured soothingly. 'He'll know soon enough. Then he'll have to eat crow.'

Kath jerked out of her arms, too upset to be comforted. 'No way! Jack doesn't eat crow. What he'll do is demand I have an abortion, and I can't——'

The tears fell again, raining down her face, and Anna's heart ached for her.

Her own pregnancy had been a disaster, an unplanned, unexpected side-effect of the most stupid and regrettable night of her life.

And yet she could never regret Flissy. Right from the beginning, her pregnancy had been a joy and a comfort to her. Career-wise, of course, it had been an unmitigated disaster, but Anna didn't care. She enjoyed her job, but she loved her little daughter passionately, and nothing and no one could ever be more important.

So she knew how Kath felt, how protective, how defensive—and how emotionally fragile.

She could feel for Jack, too—his own life ravaged by the trauma and grief of his son's short life and untimely death. No wonder he didn't want to repeat the experience!

'You could have a test to see if you're a carrier. If you're not, then the baby will be no worse off than Jack, and maybe better,' she reasoned quietly.

'And if I am?'

Anna swallowed. 'Then you have a twenty-five per cent chance that the baby will have cystic fibrosis, and a fifty per cent chance it will be a carrier. There's even a twenty-five per cent chance that it will be clear.'

Kath laughed. 'Lies, damned lies and statistics, eh, Anna? Oh, hell, what am I going to do?'

Anna passed her a tissue. 'You're going to wipe your eyes, blow your nose and come and help me with the RTA just coming in.'

Kathleen nodded, took the tissue and blew her nose noisily. 'Bloody man. I knew I shouldn't have married him. My mother said it would end in tears.'

'Kath, it hasn't ended——'

'Yet. What if it was an isolated pocket of sperm that had been lurking around?'

'For fifteen years? Come on.'

'It's no more unlikely than that the operation would fail after all this time. What if they can't find any sperm? He'll never believe me.'

Anna sighed. Kathleen was right. Please, God, it wouldn't be the case.

She heard the ambulance reversing up to the doors, its warning bleeper sounding, and hesitated.

'Go on. I'll be all right,' said Kathleen. 'I'll just wash my face and I'll be out there with you.'

Anna left her, rounding up Patrick on the way with the minimum of conversation.

The accident victims were not seriously injured, fortunately, and, after cleaning them up and putting a wrist support on the badly wrenched right arm of one driver and a collar on the neck of the other, just as a precaution, they went back into the staff-lounge together.

Jack was there, standing with his back to them, a cigarette in his hand.

He turned when they went in, and Anna was shocked at the ravaged look on his face.

Kath, in front of Anna, came to a dead halt.

'Well?' she asked bitterly.

'I'm sorry,' he said. His voice was tight with pain. 'I should have believed you.'

In front of her Anna saw Kath's shoulders sag slightly with relief. Now for the next bit.

Jack's granite eyes flicked to hers, then to Patrick's.

'Could you cover for us again? We really do need to talk.'

'Of course,' Anna agreed instantly. 'We'll manage.'

Jack stubbed the cigarette out, his fingers unsteady,

and laid his hand gently on Kath's shoulder. 'Shall we go to my office?'

She shrugged off his hand and turned on her heel, and Anna and Patrick parted to let them through. Anna watched them go, her heart aching for them. Could they sort it out? If they couldn't, she didn't know who could. God knows, they loved each other enough.

Behind her Patrick coughed to attract her attention.

She turned and met his slightly bemused eyes. 'I don't suppose you'd like to fill me in?' he asked softly.

She sighed. There was gossip, and there was sharing a problem with a friend. She weighed it up and decided that Kath and Jack probably wouldn't mind if she told him. After all, they had made no secret of their problems up to now. Damn it, Jack had even proposed to Kathleen live on national television one night! After that, discussing them in confidence with a colleague was truly small potatoes. She drew him into the room and closed the door.

'Kath's pregnant,' she said.

His eyebrows shot up. 'Pregnant? He looks as if she's just told him she's run off with his best friend!'

A sad smile flickered round Anna's mouth. 'Nothing so uncomplicated, I'm afraid.'

She filled him in briefly, and he let out a soft whistle and shook his head. 'Oh dear, oh dear. What a mess.'

'Exactly. And now they really are at an impasse, because Jack will want Kath to have an abortion, and she point-blank refuses to consider it.'

Patrick studied her for a while in silence. Then he asked, 'What do you think she should do?'

Anna's jaw dropped. 'Me? Have the baby, of course.'

'And what about the risk of CF? I can see his point. It isn't nice, Anna.'

Her mouth tightened. 'Nor is abortion.'

'No.' His eyes searched hers. 'Did you ever consider it, when you were pregnant with Flissy?'

'Not for a second,' she told him firmly, remembering her shock when a colleague had suggested it. 'Anyway, what do you think they should do?'

He shrugged. 'God knows. I just know what I'd do.'

'And that is?'

'Keep the baby and pray.'

Anna smiled. 'You're really quite a nice person, Patrick.'

'Why, thank you, Miss Jarvis. I'm honoured by your opinion.'

They shared a smile, but somewhere in the middle of it something happened, something slow and insidious that crept up on them and left them defenceless.

Patrick's smile faded, and his hand came up and cupped her jaw in its hard warmth. She could feel the strong fingers against her cheek, the slightly roughened pad of his thumb chafing lightly against the skin.

'Have dinner with me,' he murmured.

'I can't,' she whispered. 'Flissy's hand. . .'

'Tomorrow, then. Bring her to my mother's for lunch. We'll have a barbecue if it's warm. It'll take her mind off her cut.'

The stroke of his thumb was mesmerising. Her legs felt weak, her chest compressed, so that she could scarcely breathe.

'OK,' she agreed, a little raggedly.

'Good. I'll pick you up at twelve.'

'Fine.'

They stood there, trapped by each other's eyes, until the ringing in the distance finally penetrated their daze.

'Phone,' Anna said breathlessly, and, yanking open the door, she escaped from the room and those mesmerising eyes.

CHAPTER FIVE

ANNA woke the following morning wondering what on earth she'd let herself in for. One minute he was saying he hoped he hadn't given her the wrong impression when his kiss had nearly singed her socks off, the next he was asking her out to dinner and then transforming it into a family lunch to include his mother!

Frankly, she didn't know what to think or expect. She wasn't even sure that he would turn up—except he had promised her he would, with that same solemn expression he had used when he had told Flissy her hand wouldn't hurt while he stitched it, and, like Flissy, she believed him.

So here she was, at twelve o'clock, dressed casually in jeans and a soft silk shirt that had been her last birthday treat to herself. She'd dressed it up with a couple of strings of cheap but pretty beads slung round the neck, and the effect was informal but quite pleasing. After all, while she didn't want to let herself down, she didn't want Patrick thinking she was trying too hard—especially when he couldn't seem to make up his mind about the kind of relationship he wanted with her!

Her only doubt was her hair, and she twisted it up and held it, then dropped it, then twisted it up again.

No, down, surely, for a barbecue?

She turned sideways, studying it in the mirror, and her eyes dropped to her figure. He was right; she was too thin. At best her bottom could be described as neat. As for her bust—well, the only time she had had anything in that department was when she was feeding

Flissy, and remembering that brought to mind her conversation with Flissy on the subject the previous day.

Her cheeks heated at the memory of Flissy's searching questions and her cringingly frank replies. Not for anything would she have lied to Fliss, but Patrick's presence had made the conversation seem somehow far more personal.

Especially when Flissy had asked, 'Mummy, what does it feel like?'

'Wonderful,' she had replied honestly. 'Absolutely right.'

'Yes, but what does it *feel* like?' Flissy had persisted. So Anna had told her to put her finger in her mouth and suck the end hard.

'That's what it's like, except not your finger, of course, but your nipple. And luckily most babies don't have teeth at first.'

Flissy had thought about that for a second. 'Does it hurt?'

'No. Only if the baby's mouth isn't in quite the right place, but otherwise, no.'

Flissy had looked up at her and asked, 'Isn't it a bit odd?'

She had almost felt Patrick's eyes on her as she replied, but she had ignored him.

'No,' she said. 'No, it's wonderful—like a little miracle.'

Flissy had snuggled against her then, and nuzzled her small breast with her cheek.

'They don't look big enough,' she said doubtfully. 'That lady's in the picture look much bigger than yours.'

Anna had felt her cheeks flame, but had calmly explained that they grew especially for feeding babies, and then went back to their normal size afterwards.

Fortunately, before Flissy could launch off on a discussion of what constituted normal, Patrick had interrupted them to say her hand was finished. Anna's relief had been almost comic, and after a quick glance at his smothered smile she had been unable to meet his eye, diverting her attention, instead, to studying Flissy's stitches.

Flissy called her now, telling her that Patrick was outside and coming up the path, and sure enough, seconds later, the bell rang.

Giving her hair one last swipe with the brush, she ran downstairs and opened the door.

He gave an exaggerated blink. 'You're ready. I didn't think women did that.'

'Women?' she asked coolly, trying to ignore him in snug jeans and a crisp white cotton shirt that showed off his tan and his criminally sexy legs to equally good effect. 'Are we clones or something?'

He gave a rueful laugh. 'No, of course not. I'm sorry. I'm just not used to it.' He turned to Flissy and crouched down, diminishing the impact of his height just as he had yesterday. 'Hello, sweetheart. How are the stitches?'

'Sore,' she told him solemnly, and extended her hand for his inspection.

'Oh, dear. Still, they look quite well. The soreness won't last very long, poppet.'

'Kiss it better,' Flissy demanded.

He obeyed without hesitation, folding her fingers over and kissing her wrist instead of the injured palm.

'You didn't kiss it in the right place!' she said indignantly.

'Ah, but it's covered in plastic skin. It only works if you kiss the real skin, and so I had to find the nearest bit.'

Flissy studied him seriously for a second, then

nodded, as if it all made perfect sense. 'Can I bring my rabbit?' she asked then.

'Rabbit?' He looked bemused.

'Just a toy one,' Anna explained, struggling with her emotions.

'Oh, fine. Yes, of course you can bring your rabbit.'

Flissy ran off to get it and Patrick straightened up and smiled at Anna. 'She's a delightful child.'

Anna nodded, her heart full. They had looked so good together, somehow. So—right? She felt a stab of pain for Flissy that she had no father—no other family, either, come to that. Only Anna, and she was out at work.

A heavy sigh escaped, and Patrick's eyes narrowed as he looked at her. 'Is something wrong?'

She shook her head. 'No, nothing's wrong. I was just thinking about Flissy's hand,' she lied.

He didn't look convinced, but Flissy reappeared then, before he could take Anna up on it, and complete with moth-eaten rabbit they set off for Patrick's home.

It was in the country, about four miles out, a lovely whitewashed Suffolk longhouse, set in a little fold in the land with a pond next to the road surrounded by late daffodils. They turned off the road and drove past the pond, over a little bridge, and pulled up in front of the house outside a low wall with a pair of wrought-iron gates set in the centre. The wall turned at right angles at each end and ran back to the house, enclosing a small, sheltered area that Anna could see in the summer would be a riot of colour. Delicate wall-shrubs, old-fashioned roses and vigorous, hearty perennials all nestled in the shelter of the mellow brick walls, with a rose-bed in the middle of a circular gravelled area that gave access to the front door.

To the left was a small copse, and behind the house

through a gate in a high wall, Patrick told her, was the main garden.

'This is Mum's little bit,' he told her, waving his arm in the general direction of the walled area.

Little? Anna thought, and nearly laughed. Her own 'little' garden would fit into the enclosed area about twenty times over, but in front of the big house the garden looked quite manageable.

'It's lovely,' she said honestly, admiring the magnolia trees that bloomed like pale pink tulips against the dark wood of the bare branches.

'My father is the real gardener,' he told her, and something in his tone made her hesitate. He talked about his father in the present tense, and yet there had been no indication that he would be here.

Were his parents divorced? Somehow Anna didn't think so.

The front door opened just then and a delicately pretty woman with snow-white hair and a very expensive haircut came out and smiled.

'You must be Anna,' she said with a lovely smile, and, reaching out her hands, she cupped Anna's shoulders and kissed her cheek with genuine warmth.

Anna was touched, her smile a trifle wobbly. 'And you must be Mrs Haddon,' she replied.

'Maggie, please. And you're Felicity—or can I call you Flissy?'

Flissy giggled and hid behind Anna's legs. 'She's a bit shy,' Anna explained.

'Of course she is. She'll come round. Anna, perhaps you'd like to come and try the fresh lemonade I made this morning—and I do believe that the kittens might just have woken up.'

Flissy appeared from behind Anna's legs. 'Kittens?' she said, with eyes like saucers.

Maggie Haddon was clearly a very sensible woman,

Anna thought with a smile as watched her daughter go through the front door, hand in hand with her hostess.

Patrick was smiling, his face strangely sad. 'Thank you for coming. Since my father's been ill she's had a lot to contend with. She loves children, and I knew Flissy would be good for her.'

'Where is your father?' Anna asked cautiously.

Patrick sighed. 'In a home. He's got Alzheimer's disease.'

'Oh, no, Patrick, I am sorry,' Anna said spontaneously, laying her hand on his arm.

He covered it with his own large hand and squeezed gently. 'It's pretty hard-going really. He doesn't know me. I have to reintroduce myself every time I go in——'

He broke off and stared at his feet for a second. 'Sorry.' He drew a shaky breath and looked past her across the valley, his eyes clouded with pain. 'All that time together when I was a boy, all thrown away, forgotten. All the good times we had, the fun we shared. Sometimes it just gets me.'

'I'm sure,' she said softly. 'Oh, Patrick, what a shame. Does he know your mother?'

He nodded. 'Oh, yes. He recognises her, but he can't remember much of the recent past. They think he's forgotten me because I've been away so much for the past fifteen years. His memory's very patchy. Sometimes I think he's almost sorted out who I am, and then I can practically see a veil fall over his eyes and he goes all remote on me again.' He looked at her, forcing a smile that didn't reach his eyes. 'Never mind, that's my problem. Let's go and see what my mother and Flissy are doing.'

She followed him, her emotions riding very close to the surface, her awareness of his moods heightened by the unexpected glimpse of the man she had so far only guessed at.

Despite the lurking melancholy she sensed in him, it was a lovely day, the lunch a long-winded barbecue that drifted into the afternoon. As they sat in the garden, Anna noticed Flissy's eyes drifting now and then to the old grey pony grazing quietly in the paddock beside the garden.

She was wide-eyed and almost completely overawed when he ambled up and graciously allowed her to pat him, with Patrick's unobtrusive supervision.

'Would she like to sit on him?' Maggie suggested.

Flissy's eyes widened even further, but Anna chewed her lip and hesitated.

'Toby's a real gentleman,' Patrick told her quietly. 'He's thirty-six now, even older than me, and I can guarantee he won't do anything to hurt her.'

Flissy turned her little head up to Anna. 'Please, Mummy? He's so sweet. . .'

'All right, then,' she agreed reluctantly. 'If Patrick doesn't mind holding you.'

Patrick swung himself easily over the post and rail fence, and Flissy ducked through and reached up her arms trustingly to him.

He lifted her, dropped a kiss on her forehead, and settled her gently on to the old pony's back.

'Oh, he's all warm!' Flissy squeaked, and, bending forward, she patted his neck with her tiny hand. 'Good boy, Toby,' she crooned, and Patrick smiled indulgently and took Toby by the mane, one arm still round Flissy's waist.

'Come on, boy, let's go for a little wander, shall we?'

Anna watched anxiously as Patrick led Toby up the field a little way, Flissy sitting contentedly in the circle of his big arm, her curls bobbing with excitement as she chattered to Patrick.

'She'll be fine,' Maggie said quietly beside Anna. 'Toby and Patrick will look after her. They've both got a gift with children.'

Anna nodded. 'Patrick certainly has. He was wonderful with Flissy yesterday when she cut herself. I thought she'd make the most dreadful fuss.'

'It's because he's so calm and placid. He always was. Children and animals always flocked round him because he was so gentle and un-sudden. Do you know what I mean?'

She smiled. 'Yes, I do.' Her smile faded. 'Mrs Haddon, do you mind if I ask you something?'

'Of course not, dear, and it's Maggie.'

Anna smiled again faintly, warmed by her kindness. 'Maggie, then. I was wondering—when did Patrick's wife die?'

'Ah. Isobel. Hasn't he told you?'

She shook her head. 'No. Only that she has, in an earthquake at a school somewhere. Nothing else. He didn't seem to want to talk about it.'

Maggie sighed heavily. 'No, well, he doesn't. It was two years ago at Easter. They were in Mexico on holiday. It was only a fairly small earthquake, not the sort to hit the international news, but it happened while Isobel was visiting the local school. She was a teacher, and she wanted to see how the children were taught over there in the mountain villages. Patrick was devastated. I've never seen anyone so empty. He went to Africa straight after the funeral, and he didn't come home until I contacted him three months ago about his father.'

Maggie looked thoughtfully at Anna. 'He hasn't got over her, I don't think. He hasn't faced it yet. He changes the subject every time I bring it up, and watching his father slowly decline is just another wound that I'm afraid won't heal. I wish I could help him, but

I don't think I've got the weaponry.' She looked at Anna searchingly. 'I suppose I ought to warn you off, in case he hurts you, but I think in my heart of hearts I'm hoping you'll be able to break through the ice and let him out again. Just bear in mind that he isn't really whole at the moment, and you're very likely to get hurt if you don't have the sense to run.'

Anna's smile was gently wry. 'I think it's too late for that,' she confessed in a soft voice. 'Thank you for the warning, though. I'd more or less realised the situation, but, as you say, he doesn't reveal a lot, does he?'

His mother snorted softly. 'That depends on how well you know him. I know, for instance, that he finds you very attractive. I also know that he thinks it's just a case of hormones and he can ignore it, but I know Patrick. He's never had an affair just for the sake of it, and always, without fail, he's been the one who was hurt. He looks big and tough, but under that rather gruff exterior he's just a pussycat.' Maggie glanced sideways at Anna. 'If you could manage to convince him it was just physical, he might relax long enough to let you under his skin.'

Anna blushed, and instantly Maggie apologised. 'I don't know what I'm thinking about. I shouldn't be talking to you like this about my son, should I? It's just that he's hurting so much and he's so lonely, Anna—I hate to see him so lonely. He needs someone to share things with—even if they are only the physical things. He's such a passionate person, and his life's been passionless for far too long. He should have a wife and children, something to come home for at night.'

Anna, no stranger to loneliness, felt her eyes prickle with tears. If it wasn't for Flissy her life would be a wasteland. She watched as Patrick turned the pony round and they ambled slowly back across the field towards them. She waved to Flissy, and a little hand waved back.

She looked completely confident, so trusting that Anna wanted to weep. If she and Patrick had an affair, would Flissy be the one who was hurt? She'd have to make sure they didn't get too close.

'Mummy, it's wonderful!' Flissy cried as they drew nearer. 'He's so nice, isn't he?'

Toby reached his head over the fence and nuzzled Anna's pockets gently.

'He wants a mint or a carrot,' Patrick explained.

'Oh,' Anna said. 'I'm sorry,' she told Toby, 'I haven't got anything for you.' Cautiously, not used to horses or ponies, she reached up and patted his face.

He pricked his ears and regarded her steadily with honest brown eyes.

'You're a good boy, Toby,' Maggie said, and a mint appeared miraculously in her hand. He took it, crunching it up with evident enjoyment, and then nudged Maggie for another.

'No. You'll get fat and your teeth will rot.'

Patrick laughed and swung Flissy down. 'Let Fliss give him one.'

He put the mint in the centre of Flissy's good hand, showed her how to hold her fingers flat and her thumb out of the way, and while Anna held her breath and prayed for her daughter's tiny fingers, Toby delicately lifted the mint off her palm with his lips and crunched it.

Flissy looked at her hand, wrinkled her nose and wiped her palm down her dungarees. 'Yuck,' she said softly, and Patrick laughed, swinging her up on to his shoulders.

'How about a game of croquet?' he suggested as he climbed carefully over the fence, Flissy balancing herself with her hands firmly knotted in his hair.

'Good idea,' Maggie agreed.

'Oh, but surely it's time we were going?' Anna said quickly.

'Must you?' Maggie said, sounding almost disappointed.

'Do you want to go?' Patrick asked. 'I'll take you home if you like, but if you've got nothing else to do there's no reason to go yet.'

She chewed her lip. They had nothing to do— nothing, at least, that rivalled playing croquet on the lawn and listening to the humming of the bees.

'Then we'd love to stay,' she said with a smile, and so they played croquet and had a cup of tea, and then Maggie suggested they stay for an early supper, and somehow it was eight o'clock before Patrick drove her and her sleepy little daughter home.

By the time they arrived Flissy had dropped off in the back of the car, and Patrick eased her carefully out in his big arms and carried her up the path.

'Are you coming in?' Anna asked, and his eyes flicked searchingly to hers.

'Am I invited?'

'We could have a cup of coffee,' she suggested, knowing as she did how foolish that was. Patrick's mind wasn't on coffee and neither was hers, but for some foolish reason she didn't want the lovely day to come to an end quite so soon.

'How about Flissy?' he asked quietly, looking down at the sleeping child in his arms.

'She'll be fine. Just give me five minutes to put her to bed and I'll be down, OK?'

'I'll carry her up,' he offered, and so Anna led him up the narrow stairs that ran between the front and back rooms and turned into the small bedroom at the back.

'In here,' she said, and he laid Flissy down on the

bed against the wall and went out, leaving Anna to undress her daughter and slip her under the covers. Her teeth and hair could wait for one night, she decided. She'd take her to the bathroom later, if she woke.

She turned the light down and pulled the door to, then ran lightly downstairs and through to the kitchen. Patrick was spooning instant coffee into two mugs, and turned to her with a smile.

'All settled?' he asked.

She nodded. Heavens, he seemed bigger than ever in her tiny kitchen. She launched herself into conversation to cover her scattered emotions.

'It was a lovely day, wasn't it? Toby's sweet. I was a bit scared, but Flissy really seemed to enjoy herself——'

'Anna?'

She floundered to a halt and swallowed, forcing herself to meet his eyes. What she saw there did nothing to reassure her.

Her breath left her lungs in a little whoosh, and Patrick put down the kettle deliberately and closed the gap between them, drawing her into his arms.

'I've been wanting to do this all day,' he murmured, and then his lips came softly down and closed over her tiny sigh.

Oh, bliss. His touch was gentle, the stroke of his tongue against her lips mesmerising. They parted and his velvet tongue slid through the gap and found her own, playing tag with it. Then he sucked, very gently, and drew her tongue into his mouth.

A startled little moan rose in her throat and he eased her up against his solid frame, his hands warm and firm against her spine.

Her hands were against his chest, clamped in his

shirt, and she had to force herself to relax them and lay them against the heavy beat of his heart.

She felt an answering throb deep inside her body, and, sliding her arms round him, she pressed her palms against his back and wriggled closer.

A deep groan sounded in his throat and he plunged his tongue into her mouth, the act erotic and suggestive, destroying her tenuous grip on her control.

She felt his fingers tug the shirt from the waistband of her jeans and stiffened as his fingers slid up inside it and curved over the scant swell of her left breast. His hand flattened, the palm chafing against the lace of her bra, and she felt her nipple peak and strain towards his touch.

Breaking the kiss, he tugged the rest of her shirt out and raised it up, bending his head to study the pretty bra with its slight contents.

Anna's eyes slid shut, blocking the contempt she knew she would see. 'I'm sorry,' she whispered. 'I don't have a bust, really.'

'You're lovely,' he breathed, a slight catch in his voice, and her lids flew up in surprise to see his gentle eyes blaze with passion. 'Take it off, Anna. Let me look at you.'

Almost dying of fear, her hands trembling, she slid the shirt off her shoulders and unclipped the bra, letting it fall away. Now he would see how small she was, see the pathetic excuse for breasts that adorned her miserable chest. . .

'Look at me,' he commanded softly.

She did, sheer pride lifting her chin and bringing her eyes up to meet his. What she saw there wasn't contempt at all, but a tender reverence that tore at her heart.

'You're beautiful,' he said quietly. 'Quite, quite beautiful.' His hands came up and cupped her breasts softly. Unbidden, they peaked for him, and he groaned and lowered his face, drawing first one, then the other into his mouth. 'I thought I was going to die when you were talking to Flissy about breastfeeding yesterday. All I could see was you holding her to your breast, suckling her.'

He straightened, a look of longing on his face. 'I wish I could have seen you feed her,' he confessed gruffly, and her breath came in tiny gasps that lifted her aching breasts towards him again.

Gone was the shame, the humiliation. In its place was a desperate longing that only Patrick could fill.

Reaching out she unbuttoned his shirt and tugged it free of his jeans, then she moved closer until the sensitive skin of her breasts felt the soft graze of his dark curls.

His breath left him as if he'd been punched, and, tipping her chin, he kissed her with a passion she had only guessed at.

Her own need rose to meet his, and when he lifted his head in question there was only one answer.

Taking his hand, she led him up the narrow stairs and turned into her room, closing and locking the door behind her.

Then she turned back to him, her eyes wide, her breathing ragged. 'I don't know what to do next,' she confessed.

Puzzlement clouded his face. 'I don't understand.'

She flapped a hand uselessly. 'I don't do this very often—well, only once, in fact. You'll have to show me how.'

Realisation dawned, and carefully, very gently, he drew her back into his arms. 'Once?' he said incredulously.

She nodded. 'It's OK, though. I'm protected. I didn't want to risk another surprise pregnancy.'

'Are you sure?' he asked.

'Of course I'm sure. I've got an IUCD.'

He stroked her hair. 'No, I meant about us—about doing this.'

Her hand came up and cupped the back of his neck, drawing his face down to hers again. 'Oh, yes,' she told him. 'I'm sure.'

'Then I'll close the curtains before the neighbours have too much to talk about,' he said softly, and, striding away from her, he yanked the curtains closed across the window, cutting off the light from the streetlamps outside.

She turned on the bedside light as he came towards her, his eyes blazing, and drew her back into his arms.

His kiss was gentle, steady, giving her confidence and at the same time rekindling the passion that her doubts had quelled. She slid her hands over his back, feeling the firm, hot contours of his shoulders beneath her palms, revelling in the muscled strength of his body.

As her hands stroked down his back and round his sides, he groaned and stepped back. 'Hang on,' he muttered, and, kicking off his shoes, he stripped away his jeans and socks, retaining only the scanty briefs that left nothing to her imagination.

Her breath jerked in, and her eyes darted up to his, wide with surprise. He was so masculine, so potent, so—ready.

He unfastened her jeans and slid them down her legs, tugging them off her feet as she mechanically lifted one foot at a time to allow him to remove her clothes. Fear dried her mouth, but she had said she would do this and she would. . .

'Anna, it's OK,' he told her quietly. 'You can change your mind.'

She shook her head. 'No. Just hold me for a minute first, OK?'

He slipped his arms round her and eased her up against him, and that first contact with his hard, lean body shocked her right down to her toes.

Please, God, let it be better this time, she prayed. Don't let it hurt me—not like before. I love him. Surely that will make it different.

He lifted her chin and brushed her lips with his, then, easing away, he turned back the quilt and pushed her on to the bed. 'Do you want the light on or off?' he asked.

'On. I want to know it's you,' she told him through stiff lips.

He looked at her oddly, then he lifted her and set her very gently in the middle of the bed, coming down beside her and pulling the quilt over them both against the chill of the evening.

'Tell me about it,' he said.

She could feel his body against hers, hard and warm, his arousal evident and yet somehow quite unthreatening. She swallowed. 'I was twenty-one, nearly twenty-two. I'd just started work as a staff nurse. There was a party one Friday night, just like there always are. I went with my flatmates, and during the course of the evening I had a bit too much to drink. This doctor I vaguely knew came on to me a bit, and I thought, What the hell? Everyone else does. My virginity was beginning to be a bit of a burden, so when he suggested we went upstairs I agreed.'

'And?' he prompted, when she paused before the difficult bit.

'It was awful. It hurt dreadfully, and afterwards he just got up without a word and went downstairs again. I got dressed and went down a little later, and I overheard him talking to a friend.'

Her mouth clamped into a grim line and she bit her lip.

'What did he say, Anna?' Patrick asked softly.

She took a deep breath. 'He said it was the hardest tenner he'd ever earned in his life, and he'd seen bigger bumps on an ironing-board.'

She felt him stiffen, his body rigid with anger. 'Bastard,' Patrick hissed against her hair. 'Does he know about Flissy?'

She shook her head. 'No. I thought she deserved a better start in life.'

'Quite right, too. He doesn't deserve her.' His arms closed round her, holding her against his broad, solid chest, and she turned into his embrace and clung to him until the memory faded, replaced by the musky scent of his skin and the warmth of his breath against her cheek.

'Anna?' he murmured.

She tipped her head back, seeking his mouth, and seconds later her fear was a thing of the past. His kiss was tender, searching, giving, making her quiver with need deep inside.

For a long time he just kissed her, his hands still against her shoulders, but then as she moaned and arched against him, one hand slid slowly down her side and eased her up against him so that she could feel the hard imprint of his arousal against her thigh. She moved against it and a deep groan erupted from his throat.

'I want to touch you,' she whispered.

'Help yourself,' he replied, but his voice was ragged and his breath caught as her hand slid over his hip and brushed against the straining briefs.

'Anna,' he breathed as she slipped her hand under the elastic and touched him tentatively. She grew bolder, dragging a shuddering sigh from him as her fingers closed round him, then he pulled her hand away, his body trembling. 'Take it steady,' he said gruffly. 'I'm so close.'

His hands moved over her again, drawing her lacy pants down over her legs and then sliding back up, caressing the delicate skin of her inner thigh until his fingers brushed lightly against the damp nest of curls that ached for his touch.

She bucked against his hand, her eyes widening, and he moved over her, positioning himself carefully. She tensed slightly, her heart racing. Would it be all right this time? Oh, dear, God, please. . .

Then he paused and stared searchingly into her eyes. 'Anna?'

She could hardly breathe. 'Yes?' she whispered.

'Be gentle with me,' he said earnestly.

For a moment she was stunned, then a soft gust of laughter escaped her. 'You're crazy,' she told him, and the laughter bubbled up, foaming over as he held her and washing away the tension inside.

Then as the laughter faded so tension returned, but a different tension now, less desperate, all shadows banished to the past. His smile faded too, leaving just the kindness in his eyes that slowly gave way to a raging need.

She lifted a hand and touched his face tenderly. 'Please,' she breathed, and the next instant she felt a wonderful, completing fullness as their bodies joined.

He gave her a moment to adjust, then started moving slowly, unhurriedly, despite the fierce need she could sense in him.

In her, too. 'Patrick,' she cried, stunned by the ripples of sensation that were already spreading through her.

'Oh, yes, Anna,' he grated, and, lifting himself on

his hands, he looked down at her as he moved slowly, deeply inside her.

Her throat tightened, the blood pounding in her ears, and then he was moving harder, faster, and suddenly the ripples spread, fanning out until her whole body was aflame.

She cried out, reaching for him, and with a guttural cry his arms buckled and he fell against her, his body shuddering as his massive control shattered and he gave in to the wild sensation that swept them both in its path.

As the wildness eased and peace followed, she smoothed the sweat-slicked skin of his back and held him against her heart.

She loved him—loved him even as she loved Flissy, with the same passionate intensity and desperate loyalty. Tears filled her eyes but she blinked them away. He mustn't know. She must pretend it was just sex or she'd frighten him away before she could soothe the pain in his heart and make him whole again.

Only then would he truly be hers.

CHAPTER SIX

HE DIDN'T stay for coffee.

Anna, unused to coping with the aftermath of her emotions, was actually quite grateful to be alone with her thoughts.

She watched him go, her lips still tingling from his goodbye kiss, and then she wandered into the kitchen and made herself a cup of tea, taking it through to the little sitting-room and curling up among Flissy's scattered toys on the sofa, her mind tumbling the events of the past few hours over and over to try and make sense of them.

He had been so gentle, that little touch of humour all that was needed to drive away the last of her demons. How had he known that? And later, when his body was clamouring, he had held back, waiting for her.

She scrubbed the moisture from her cheeks and sniffed hard. Damn. Well, she'd thought he'd be a sensitive lover. Now she knew. If only he'd said those three little words.

She scrubbed at the tears again. Don't be daft, she told herself sternly. It's less than a week since you met him. Of course he doesn't love you!

It didn't alter the fact that she loved him—probably had from the moment he yanked her out of the cab and crushed her against his chest on Thursday. Or was it from Monday, when he had fed her sandwiches and warm doughnuts?

Or even before, when she had heard that wonderful laugh. . .?

She sighed. It was academic. The process had probably been gradual, starting with the laugh and steadily building until now she felt she could die from loving him.

Cross with herself, she smacked down her mug on the table and stood up, scooping Flissy's toys into her arms and chucking them anyhow into the toy-box.

'You're a fool,' she lectured herself aloud. 'You heard his mother. Even she told you you ought to run while she was begging you not to. You should have listened, not dragged him straight back here and into bed with such indecent haste. Oh, hell. . .'

She rummaged in her dressing-gown pocket for a tissue and swiped at her eyes. 'Idiot. He's still hung up on his wife—probably shut his eyes and pretended you were her.'

Except he hadn't. She knew that because she had been watching him all the time, their eyes locked, and at the end it had been Anna's name on his lips.

OK, so he had known it was her. That didn't mean he loved her, or that he was about to fall in love with her. It probably meant nothing more than that he had good manners and tried to remember the name of the woman currently in his arms——

She hurled a cushion across the room and stomped up to bed. That didn't help. The sheets were rich with the fragrance of his skin, the air heavy with memories.

She wouldn't sleep a wink. With a sigh she went in to Flissy and lifted her out of bed, taking her to the bathroom and then carrying her back to bed, still almost asleep.

Then she went and climbed into bed, snuggled down in the sheets that had surrounded their passion and thought of Patrick.

Despite the sorrow she knew was coming, her heart was filled with warmth and gentleness. She closed her eyes and breathed in his scent, and desire teased her senses.

She gave herself up to the memories.

Monday was chaos. Anna supposed that because Friday had been so quiet, they had had it coming.

Fortunately, Greg Warren, their SHO, was back from his holiday. Good job, Anna thought, as she rushed from one patient to another.

She saw Patrick briefly and very publicly, and was profoundly grateful that there wasn't time to speak. She had no idea what to say to him, how to play it, where they went from here. Maybe she ought to ask his mother, she thought with wry humour.

Her reprieve didn't last. Before long they were side by side, working on a young lad with multiple abrasions.

'What on earth were you doing?' Patrick asked him, eyeing the torn and bleeding skin that covered almost all his legs and back.

'Skateboarding,' he told them.

Patrick raised a disbelieving eyebrow. 'Oh, yeah?'

The lad looked even more uncomfortable. 'Behind a car. We've done it before. You lie on the board and the car drags it along. It's really good fun.'

Patrick gave his injuries a considering look. 'I can see that,' he said drily.

The lad shrugged and then gave a little grunt of pain. 'I fell off and my foot got caught in the tow-rope somehow.'

'And you were dragged?'

He nodded. 'Not far. Only a couple of hundred metres.'

'Only?' Patrick muttered. 'How fast was your friend going?'

.

'About thirty. Eventually he heard me yelling and stopped.'

Patrick sighed. 'You'll need skin-grafts to cover some of those wounds, and I'm afraid you'll have some scarring.'

He looked up at Anna. 'He'll have to go to Theatre to have the wounds debrided. We can't tackle all of him without a GA.'

'What's a GA?' the lad asked, looking apprehensive.

'A general anaesthetic,' Patrick told him. 'Your wounds all need cleaning up before the extent of the damage can be assessed. Only then can we see just how bad your injuries are, but we have to get all the grit and dirt and bits of cloth out of your skin.'

Patrick glanced at Anna again. 'He'll need a tetanus booster as well. You'd better see to that.'

She nodded. His eyes had revealed little that helped her to gauge his emotions, to work out how he felt about Saturday night. Not knowing how to react to him, she carried on as if nothing had happened, all brisk professionalism.

She found a relatively clean piece of skin on the upper arm, gave the boy the tetanus booster and then his mother arrived, looking frantic.

'What the devil did you think you were playing at?' she yelled. 'You were supposed to be at college! I've told you and told you about fooling around like that behind a car—well, perhaps you'll listen to me now. Look at you!'

And she burst into tears. Anna comforted her, gave her a cup of tea and talked her down a little, then Patrick explained what they would have to do and the likely outcome of the injuries.

The plastic surgeon came and examined him, tutted copiously, and then he was wheeled off to Theatre, his mother trailing miserably.

Anna found herself alone with Patrick in the empty cubicle, and busied herself with the debris from the young man's treatment.

His quiet voice stopped her.

'Look at me.'

She turned slowly, reluctantly, and met his eyes. The impersonal look was gone. Instead they were warm, gentle, full of memory. 'How are you?' he asked softly.

'I'm fine,' she said, her breath strangely absent.

'Good.' He stepped closer and cupped her jaw in his palm, his thumb doing disturbing things to her cheek. 'I was going to ring you but I couldn't find your number in the book.'

'No. I haven't got a phone; I can't afford it,' she explained.

'I wondered.' His thumb was turning her bones to mush, and she found herself turning her face into his hand and pressing her lips to his palm.

He swore softly, and then drew her into his arms.

'I wasn't going to touch you,' he muttered. 'I was going to be strong and professional and leave you alone, but I can't. I keep seeing you as you were on Saturday, your eyes wide with passion, making all those incredible little noises——' He broke off and swallowed, the muscles working in his jaw, and she watched in fascination as he struggled with himself.

Then, 'What the hell,' he mumbled, and, lowering his head, he took her lips in a kiss so gentle, so meltingly tender that she thought she would collapse.

Her little cry was lost in his mouth, and as he deepened the kiss his arms eased her closer so she could feel his need. God knows where the kiss would have ended, she thought, if Greg Warren hadn't stuck his head round the curtain.

There was a muttered expletive, an apology, and the sound of his retreating footsteps.

Patrick released her slowly, his blazing eyes touched now with humour. 'Oops,' he whispered.

She laughed, as she was meant to, and he moved away from her, a smile of frustration and rueful regret playing around his full, sensuous mouth.

'I'll go and find out what he wanted. You finish up here, OK?'

She nodded, and he pulled her back into his arms, hugged her briefly and then was gone.

So much for pretending nothing had happened on Saturday!

She found Kath in the office a little while later, catching up on paperwork in a little lull. She closed the door and looked at her thoughtfully.

'You look awful,' she told her bluntly.

'Thanks,' Kath said with a faint smile. 'I feel much better for knowing that.'

Anna gave her shoulder a reassuring squeeze and perched on the desk, looking down at her friend in concern.

'How are things, or daren't I ask?'

Kath sighed and leant back, ramming her hands in her pockets. 'Things are lousy, thank you. He's apologised, he's accepted the baby is his, he's booked another vasectomy with a urologist friend for this Friday evening, and he wants me to have an abortion. Well, no, that's not strictly fair. He doesn't want me to; he says it's our only option.'

'And you disagree?'

'Of course. I had a test on Friday to see if I could be a carrier, but I'm sure I'm not. The result of that will come back fairly soon.'

'If you're not, the worst case is that the baby will be a carrier of the gene, isn't it?'

Kathleen nodded. 'Yes. No worse off than Jack. We

then have the difficult task of telling our baby that he or she shouldn't really have children, unless medical science has caught up with CF by then. Can you imagine doing that?'

Anna couldn't. How would she feel if it was Flissy?

Terrible, was how. She shared a sad smile with Kathleen and slipped off the desk.

'I'm there if you need me. Any time you need to talk, just come round.'

'Thanks.' Kath looked up at her and quirked a brow. 'By the way, what's this I hear about you and the SR?'

Anna blushed. 'God, the bongos have been at it promptly.'

Kath chuckled. 'Greg said he interrupted you just before your clothes caught fire.'

Anna's cheeks burned even hotter. 'Oh, hell. I'll have to bribe him.'

'I doubt if you can afford to. He's getting so much fun out of it the premium will be very high!'

Anna gave a rueful laugh. 'Oh, blow him. Let him talk. It was just a kiss.'

'That,' Kath said drily, 'is not the way I heard it.'

'Hmm. I'll go and do some Triage.'

Kathleen's soft laugh followed her up the corridor.

There was a lull mid-afternoon, and Anna took the opportunity to slip up to Orthopaedics and see Nigel Ward, the lorry driver who had been trapped in his cab.

She found him lying in state, his injured leg resting in a gutter on traction, his right arm suspended from a sling, surrounded by flowers, cards, chocolates and visitors.

She almost turned away, but then he caught her eye and called her over.

'Hey, Anna! How you doing?'

She picked her way between the chairs and took his left hand, giving it a squeeze. 'You're looking a bit better,' she said with a smile.

'Yeah, well, that isn't difficult.' He looked at his visitors. 'This is the nurse who saved my life,' he told them, and Anna laughed a little awkwardly.

'Don't overdo it,' she said wryly. 'The other people there had something to do with it as well.'

He waved his hand dismissively, and as he met her eyes, Anna saw his fill. 'You did save my life, whatever you say. I've been wanting to thank you.'

Her vision blurred, and, bending over, she dropped a light kiss on his cheek. 'Any time,' she said a little unevenly, and then she turned and made her way out of the ward, blinking hard.

Mary O'Brien, the ward sister, stopped her on the way out. 'Well, hello there,' she said with a smile. 'You're quite the hero, my love.'

'Oh, Sister, not you too!' she said with a little embarrassed laugh. 'I only did what anyone would have done.'

Mary chuckled. 'Of course you did. You might as well enjoy the fuss, though!'

Anna's smile relaxed. 'I suppose there must be some rewards.'

'For his wife, certainly. She's pregnant—did he tell you that?'

Anna felt the warmth steal into her heart. Because of her actions, a child would grow up with a father. She had only done what her training had prepared her for, but still the result was the same, and she felt she had earned the right to be alive.

It put a spring in her step as she made her way back down to A and E, and the smile she gave Patrick was dazzling.

'You look happy,' he said, returning the smile.

'I am. I've just been to see Nigel Ward.'

Patrick pushed a set of X-ray plates up on to the light-box and squinted at them. 'How is he?'

'Fine. His wife's pregnant.'

'That was quick.'

She laughed. 'Idiot.'

He shot her a grin. 'So you're feeling good about yourself?'

'Mmm.' She moved closer and peered at the plates. They were of a hand, badly mangled, with several fractures.

'What's this?'

'Accident at work—unguarded machinery. Looks like it may have to come off. The soft tissue damage is much worse than the bone.'

'Oh, dear,' she said. She looked again at the plates. It was a right hand, of course. Industrial accidents to the hand usually involved the right rather than the left, because people used their dominant hands unthinkingly, almost by reflex. 'Do you need me?'

Patrick grinned. 'Not in the sense you mean. Kath's in there with him.'

She rolled her eyes, and with a low chuckle he pulled the X-rays out of the light-box and went back out into the corridor. As he went back to the cubicle Anna glanced in, and saw Kathleen looking distinctly sickly. She followed Patrick in.

'I'll take over,' she said firmly, and after a second's hesitation Kath muttered her thanks and fled.

Patrick glanced at her in puzzlement. 'Queasy,' she explained economically.

'Ah.'

Anna could see why. The patient's hand was, indeed, a mess. He had been caught in a roller, and the skin had been pulled down and stripped away from several of his fingers. He was doped to the eyebrows but still

moaning gently, and she checked the drip in his other
arm and wiped his head comfortingly with a cool damp
cloth.

'Just hang on, you're doing really well.'

'So stupid,' he mumbled. 'Can't believe I did it.'

His wife arrived, and Anna rigged a cradle over his
hand and draped blankets round it before showing her
in. It looked horrific enough when you were used to it,
she thought, and there was no point in adding to their
misery.

Nick Davidson came down then, and ushered the
man's wife out before turning back the blankets.

His face expressionless, he turned the hand over very
gently, studying both aspects before laying it very
carefully back down.

Patrick raised an eyebrow at him, but Nick shook his
head almost imperceptibly. Good though he was, Anna
knew there was only so much that could be done, and
with such extensive degloving of the skin the damage
to the underlying tissues would be permanent and
irreversible.

Nick called the patient's wife back in, explained the
situation, and told them he was taking him to Theatre
immediately and would see if there was any way he
could save the hand.

'I have to say I'm not hopeful,' he told them gently.
'I'll do everything I can, but I'm not God, and there
are limits to what we can achieve.'

'But they sew things back on all the time!' his wife
said desperately. 'Surely this must be easier?'

Nick shook his head. 'The sort of damage your
husband's hand has sustained is much worse than a
clean cut. I'm sorry. If you go with Staff Nurse Jarvis,
here, she'll give you the consent forms to sign for the
operation, and we'll get straight on with it. I promise
you I'll save it if I possibly can.'

After they had left the department Anna turned to Patrick. 'Do you think he stands a chance of waking up with his hand?'

Patrick shook his head. 'No—but I'm prepared to be proved wrong.'

He was—to a degree. Nick rang down later and told them he'd managed to save all but two of the fingers, and hoped that the nerve damage would prove reversible given time. 'It may not be totally useless. If it is, we'll take it off later and he can have a decent prosthesis, but we'll give it a chance.'

Anna thanked him for ringing, then passed on the information to Patrick just before she went off duty.

'Well, I said I was prepared to be proved wrong, and you did say he was good.' He hesitated for a moment, then went on, 'Are you busy tonight?'

Her heart thumped at the sudden change of topic. 'No—not really. I have to collect Fliss and cook for us, then we usually watch television or play a game or two together until her bedtime. The usual boring stuff.'

Actually she didn't really think it was boring, but she was sure Patrick would. Little children weren't everybody's cup of tea.

'Why don't we go out?' he suggested. There, she was right, he didn't want to spend time with Fliss, she thought. But then he confounded her argument. 'How about letting me take you both out for a meal?' he offered quietly, just as she was about to protest that she couldn't leave her little girl again after being out at work all day.

Anna was desperately tempted. She knew just how little food there was in the house, and the thought of cooking after her hectic day had about as much appeal as cold spaghetti, but she didn't want Fliss getting too attached to Patrick. As it was he was all she'd talked about all Sunday.

'I'm sorry, I don't think that would be a good idea,' she told him, rather bluntly because of her disappointment.

His face became impassive, unreadable, and she instantly regretted her words. 'Patrick, please don't misunderstand,' she said quickly, before he could walk away. 'It's just that I know this relationship won't last, and I don't want Flissy to get too dependent on you. I'd hate her to be hurt just because I decided to have an affair with you.'

The cold expression on his face faded. 'No, of course not. I'm sorry, I didn't think. It was just that Saturday was such fun, I thought she might enjoy it if we went out again.'

'I'm sure she would,' Anna said gently. 'That's the trouble, Patrick. We're worlds apart. I'm a single mother, struggling on a nurse's salary to pay a child-minder, living expenses and the rent on a very modest little house, and somehow keep my car on the road when I can, and you live in that wonderful house——'

'My parents' house,' he reminded her softly.

'And drive that very expensive car——'

'My father's.'

'And I don't want Flissy getting too used to it, because there's no way on earth I'll ever be able to compete.'

She floundered to a halt while he studied her, his eyes hooded and unrevealing. 'Does that mean we can't see each other either, except at work?'

Anna swallowed. The same drawbacks to their relationship applied to her as to Flissy. She didn't want to get too used to all that Patrick took for granted. She didn't want to come to rely on his company, or find the days dragging when he wasn't a part of them.

She sighed softly. It was already too late for that, as far as she was concerned. If Patrick wasn't part of her day, then the sun might as well not bother to rise. She had discovered that yesterday.

'No,' she replied. 'Of course it doesn't mean that.'

'So could I come round later? Perhaps at nine?'

Their eyes locked, the message clear.

'Yes,' she said slowly. 'Yes, do. Make it eight-thirty; she's always in bed by then.'

'Shall I bring us a take-away?'

She shook her head. 'No, or Flissy will wonder why I'm not eating. I won't tell her you're coming round.'

'A secret tryst?' he said wryly.

Anna sighed. 'Patrick, please try to understand.'

His hand cupped her cheek. 'I do. I'm just behaving like a spoilt brat. I'll see you later.'

She managed to get Flissy into bed by eight-fifteen, and was just creeping out of the bedroom door at eight-thirty when the doorbell rang. Damn. She might have known he would be prompt. She had wanted to clear up the sitting-room a little. . .

She tiptoed down the stairs and opened the front door with her finger on her lips.

Patrick was standing there, a bunch of lilac in one hand, a bottle of wine in the other. He handed her the flowers.

'I know it's supposed to be bad luck to bring lilac into the house,' he said very quietly, 'but I'm not superstitious and it was so lovely. I hope you don't mind.'

'Mind?' She buried her nose in the heavily scented blooms and breathed deeply. 'Oh, Patrick, it's heavenly. Thank you. Come in. I've just got Fliss off to sleep.'

He followed her into the kitchen, the scene of her downfall on Saturday night, and as she reached up for some wine-glasses his arms slipped round her waist and tugged her gently back against him.

'Come here,' he murmured against her hair, and she turned in his arms and gave herself up to the kiss.

Finally he lifted his head, and she gave a rather ragged smile.

'Hi,' he said gruffly.

'Hi yourself,' she managed breathlessly.

'I've been dying to finish that kiss ever since Greg walked in on us this morning,' Patrick confessed, and the memory brought the heat to Anna's cheeks.

'Everyone knows,' she told him.

He held her a little further away and looked down searchingly into her eyes. 'Do you mind?'

'Not really. I'm just not used to it.'

'No. I'm sorry. I'll be more circumspect in future. You'll have to stay on the other side of the examination couch or something.'

She smiled faintly. There was little point in telling him that the damage was done. Oh, so what? It was only her reputation, and let's face it, she thought, that was shot to shreds.

She turned and reached for the glasses again, and handed him a corkscrew. 'Here, I'll let you show off while I put the lilac in water. It really does smell wonderful.'

'It grows outside my bedroom window,' he told her, and her mind immediately conjured up an image of him sprawled across a big bed, the scent of lilac mingling with the warm musk of his skin. Her fingers trembling slightly, she put the heady white blooms in a pretty jug she had found in a junk shop.

Either because of her distraction or because she had never been very good at it, they refused to stay where she put them. By the time she had arranged them to her satisfaction Patrick had opened the wine and poured two glasses and was standing waiting, a knowing smile on his lips.

'We'll go in the sitting-room,' she said, to cover her confusion, and led him down the little hall.

They settled themselves on the sofa in the still-chaotic room, closing the curtains against prying eyes and switching on the little lamps that somehow made it all look less dreary.

'It's pretty grim, isn't it?' Anna said with a wave at the décor. 'It would have been tidy but Flissy wanted another story.'

'I was just thinking how cosy and homely it was,' he said quietly. 'I've lived in far worse in my time—far worse.'

'Like Africa?' she prompted gently, not wishing to raise a delicate subject but desperate to know more about the man she loved.

His smile was faint. 'Yes, like Africa. That was terrible—hot, dry, unforgiving. It never rained, and everything was always full of dust, great clogging, choking clouds of it every time there was a breeze. I lived in a hut about fifteen feet in diameter that doubled as the clinic. Being able to lie down straight was a luxury out there.'

Her forefinger idly traced the top of her glass. 'What were you doing there?'

'Working in a famine relief outpost. They couldn't afford a proper hospital, or even a doctor, really. I used the money I got from Isobel's life insurance to fund myself while I was there. Unfortunately it had all but run out when my mother contacted me to say my father was deteriorating, and I thought when I left that would be the end of medical help for all those poor people.'

His mouth tipped at the side. 'I was wrong. Just three weeks after I left they got the long-awaited funding for a little hospital, including the salaries for two doctors and three nurses. That means they can now do operations because they've got anaesthetic cover, which is a huge benefit in such an isolated rural area.'

'No wonder you get so frustrated here with all the throw-away packs we use these days.'

'Don't. I know it's cheaper, but it seems criminal to throw the things away when out there they'd give their eye-teeth for our cast-offs. You know, people used to spend their miserable life-savings just to reach me. It tore me to pieces when there was nothing I could do, and it happened so often. Their only hope was to travel further, to one of the cities, but they had no money to get there. Sometimes they'd walk for days—maybe weeks—to get to me, and by then it might be too late. Even if it wasn't I couldn't always help because of the difficulty of obtaining supplies. We would run out of something simple like penicillin, and children would die because of it. That really gets you.'

'I can imagine,' Anna said softly. 'To have to stand back and watch that happen. . .'

He gave a humourless little laugh. 'I got used to bribing officials and sweet-talking secretaries and finding supplies on the black market, but it was like sticking your finger in a dyke. Still, they're OK now. I gather things are beginning to shape up really well for them.'

She regarded him thoughtfully. 'You're one of those rare things—a genuinely good person,' she said softly.

His laugh was embarrassed. 'Rubbish,' he dismissed. 'I just did what needed to be done.'

'Perhaps that's what I mean.'

His fingers threaded through hers and he lifted her hand to his lips. 'You're wrong,' he said softly. 'Just now my motives are far from pristine, and my intentions don't bear inspection at all.'

Her mouth curved. 'Don't tell me—you want me for my money?'

The laughter showed in his eyes. 'Shucks, you guessed,' he murmured, then, easing her closer, he lowered his mouth to hers.

The kiss started gently, but as the passion caught them up in its fury he groaned deep in his throat and lifted his head. 'I need you,' he said raggedly.

She cupped his cheek. 'I need you, too.'

She slid her feet to the floor and stood up, pulling him up beside her. Without a word she led him upstairs, locked the door and turned to him.

The dim glow of the streetlights barely penetrated the room, but there was just enough light to see him. Eyes locked, they shed their clothes and reached for each other, their passion spiralling wildly.

They didn't speak. Words seemed unnecessary.

Bathed in the ghostly light that slanted through the window, they touched and sought, lips, hands, bodies clinging as the wild passion wreaked its havoc with their senses.

Then, slaked, they lay for a while in each other's arms, neither willing to break the silence or the contact.

Finally Patrick raised his head and kissed her tenderly.

'I ought to go before the neighbours start to talk,' he murmured.

Her smile was sad. 'They already think I'm a scarlet woman. There's nothing you could do that would make it any worse.'

'We should never judge,' he said quietly. 'So many people would have taken the easy way out.'

'I couldn't. Fliss was the only good thing to come out of that disastrous experience. That's why I called her Felicity. It means lucky.'

His smile was tender. 'She is—lucky to have you for her mother. You're one of those rare things—a genuinely good person,' he told her, quoting her own words back at her.

She laughed, embarrassed. 'Nonsense. I'm just a mother, doing what any mother does for her child.'

'Maybe,' he murmured. He kissed her again, then swung his legs over the side of the bed and quickly tugged on his clothes.

She put her dressing-gown on and followed him down.

'Do you want another coffee?' she offered.

He shook his head. 'No. I'm on call tomorrow. I ought to get as much sleep as I can tonight, and if I stay much longer I'll get side-tracked again.'

The smile was tender and full of wry humour, and Anna's lips curved in response.

'Very likely,' she told him, and with another stolen kiss he opened the door and let himself out.

She went back to the sitting-room to tidy up, and her nose caught the scent of the lilac. Again she saw him in his bedroom, the scent of lilac all around. On an impulse she took the flowers up to her own bedroom, buried her nose in the sheets and breathed Patrick and the lilac until she fell asleep.

CHAPTER SEVEN

AFTER that night they fell into a sort of loose pattern. There was never any commitment, no suggestion that he would come round without fail, but more often than not, when he wasn't on call for the night, Patrick would appear after Flissy was in bed, and they would spend the evening together.

They talked endlessly about almost anything, and Anna discovered he was a marvellous raconteur, as well as a wonderful listener.

He also talked at length about his father, who he had brought home in the care of an agency nurse. He was much happier, Patrick said, but still didn't know him. Anna could tell how much that hurt, and offered silent comfort.

However, she talked a little of her own life, about the loss of her parents, and the grandmother who had raised her single-handed and with very old-fashioned values, and whose harsh words at Flissy's birth had cut deeper than even Anna could bear to admit.

She had been surprised at the depth of her grief when the old woman had died the following year. The pain had been possibly made worse by the rift that had come between them, and she had found the funeral very hard.

Eliza's friends had stared at her, the scarlet woman, instrument of her grandmother's greatest sorrow, and she had left quietly after the service. She hadn't been back. The house contents had been sold, the trust fund from her parents handed over to her—or what was left of it.

In accordance with her parents' wishes she had been educated at a private boarding-school at considerable expense. The left-overs of her inheritance had been enough to buy her little second-hand car and a few sticks of furniture.

Still, she managed more or less, and they were happy—particularly now that Patrick was a part of her life.

Flissy still talked about him. 'When can we see him again?' she asked wistfully time after time. 'He said I could ride the pony.'

Finally Anna relented. What harm could it do, just occasionally?

After all, just because they saw him and his mother from time to time didn't necessarily mean that Fliss was going to attach herself to him as a father-figure.

Did it?

Anna hoped not. It would make such a pleasant change to spend part of the weekend with him. Those two days always seemed endless without him there. The next time he asked her, she decided, she would say yes.

Work in the A and E department continued as ever, in fits and starts. Kathleen was feeling better now, the nausea wearing off, but Jack was still not reconciled.

On the Friday at the end of Patrick's fourth week at the hospital, when Kathleen was fourteen weeks pregnant, she told Anna that she had decided to have the amniocentesis test done.

'I know now that I'm not a carrier, but Jack's so uptight about the possibility of the baby being a carrier, and there's a fifty-fifty chance it isn't, so I'm going to have it done even though there's a risk. Then I can put his mind at rest.'

Anna knew how much that decision meant to Kathleen. There was a slight chance, after the procedure to draw off a small sample of the amniotic fluid from around the baby, that the mother would go into labour. Now Jack had had another vasectomy there was no possibility of any further children, and so this really was Kath's only chance.

Knowing how much Flissy meant to *her*, Anna could only applaud Kathleen's courage. In the circumstances she didn't think she would have been so brave.

'Is Jack on this weekend?' Anna asked.

'Yes—until Sunday afternoon. Patrick's got Sunday night and Monday.'

'Why don't you go away on Sunday night? Spend some time together.'

Kath gave a short, humourless laugh. 'Time together? The way he is at the moment I'm not sure I *want* to spend time with him. He's smoking again, every now and then he hits the bottle—and anyway, he's going caving on Monday. On the bike.'

Anna was appalled. 'What? I thought he'd given all those things up.'

Kath snorted. 'So did I, Anna—so did I.'

Just then Greg Warren called Kathleen and, with a weary shake of her head, she left Anna and went to see what he wanted.

Anna, with nothing critical to do, found herself more and more angry.

She went down the corridor to where she could hear Jack's voice. He was talking to Patrick, and looked up when she approached.

'Are you looking for me?' Patrick asked.

She shook her head. 'No, Jack, actually. Could I have a word please? In private?'

Jack studied her for a second, then shrugged away from the wall. 'Sure. Come in my office.'

She followed him, her hands suddenly clammy.

Whatever was she doing? It was hardly her business, after all——

'What can I do for you?' he asked with an encouraging smile.

She wiped her hands surreptitiously on her dress and met his eyes. They looked strained, she thought, and she had a sudden surge of compassion. It must have been terrible, losing his son to such a cruel disease.

'I wanted to talk to you about Kath,' she began.

Instantly his face lost its friendly cast, and he turned away.

'What about her?'

Anna hesitated for a second, then rushed in. 'Why are you punishing her? It's hardly her fault that she's pregnant.'

'Did I say it was?' he asked harshly.

As he reached for a cigarette, his hands trembling, Anna realised that he was blaming himself, and the burden was all the harder for it.

She laid a hand on his shoulder and squeezed gently. 'It isn't your fault, either. The chances of this happening are so slight, surely, that no one could have predicted it. Why don't you look on it as a blessing, a gift you never dared to hope for?'

He turned on her, his eyes blazing. 'A gift? Watching another child die?'

She stood her ground, despite the anger in his eyes. She knew he wouldn't hurt her. 'Yes, a gift,' she said softly. 'This child won't die. At the worst it will be a carrier. By the time it's grown up, medical science may be able to offer more hope.'

Jack sighed and drew deeply on the cigarette. 'I'm sorry. It's just that this has brought back a lot of painful memories. I know the baby will be all right.'

'So why torture Kathleen?'

His brow knitted in a frown. 'Torture?'

'The bike, going caving this weekend—the cigarettes. . .'

He looked down at the spiral of smoke drifting off the cigarette in his hand, and with a sigh he stubbed it out. 'I'd given up,' he confessed.

'I know. She says you're drinking again, as well. Jack, she's worried about you.'

He swallowed hard. 'Yes, I know she is. I'll go and talk to her.'

He headed for the door but she stopped him with a hand on his arm. 'Jack? Why haven't you got rid of the bike? It really scares her. And the caving.'

He sighed softly. 'I know. It's just a form of escapism.'

'But you have responsibilities now. Don't you think you should respect them?'

His smile was wry. '*Et tu, Brute*? How much did she pay you?'

Anna laughed softly. 'She doesn't know I'm talking to you. I think she'd probably kill me. And another thing——'

He groaned. 'Yes?'

'The amniocentesis.'

He went still. 'What amniocentesis?'

Anna blinked. He didn't know? 'She said she's going to have it done to set your mind at rest.'

He swore comprehensively. 'Over my dead body will she have amniocentesis,' he muttered. 'It's too risky for the baby.'

'It isn't very risky.'

'It is when it's your only chance,' he replied softly. He put his arms round her and gave her a hard, heartfelt hug. 'Bless you for telling me. It must have taken guts to confront me; I can be a crabby old cuss when something's got to me.'

Anna gave a startled laugh. 'You can? Jack, I hadn't noticed!' she teased.

He released her with a smile and, dropping the cigarette packet in the bin, he went out of the door, whistling softly.

Anna heaved a sigh of relief and followed him out.

They were called out later that morning to a road traffic accident involving two cars on a quiet country lane. The collision had been so violent that the driver of one of the cars was reported as dead, the other driver was very seriously injured and there were two passengers in the first car who had sustained varying degrees of injury, possibly serious.

All were trapped, and a medical team was requested. As before, Patrick and Anna went together, and Patrick threatened Anna.

'No more damned heroics, do you hear me?'

She smiled benignly. 'Of course not. Would I?'

He gave a rude snort, but let it go in favour of another topic.

'I gather you gave Jack an ear-bashing this morning.'

She turned to face him. 'How on earth did you know that?' she asked in surprise.

'He told me. Actually, he sounded quite proud of you.'

'Proud?' She laughed. 'You amaze me.'

Patrick shot her a grin. 'He said you'd reminded him that he had responsibilities. He rang the paper and put the bike in the For Sale column, and he isn't going caving on Monday. He's taking Kathleen away for a couple of nights instead.'

'Wonders will never cease,' she said softly.

'Apparently. Right, you need to read those instructions. What road did they say it was on?'

They found the accident site quite easily, although it

was difficult to get very close because of the number of emergency vehicles. Patrick parked as close as he could, and they carried their equipment through the field alongside the road, rather than scramble through the rough growth between the road and the hedges.

'Fancy doing any speed at all along this lane,' Patrick said as they approached the cars. 'Look at them! They must have been tanking!'

They pushed through a gap in the hedge and slithered down the bank to the cars. One of them was a lovely old vintage car, now mangled probably beyond repair. The other was a VW Golf GTi. Patrick snorted.

'Ah, the medic,' the ambulanceman in charge said as they reached the road, and his faced registered relief. 'Bit of a nasty one, this. Young man in the old jalopy's dead, his two passengers in the rear are both quite serious, and the other driver's not doing too well.'

'Right, let's do a bit of Triage,' Patrick suggested. 'Who's making the most noise?'

'The driver of the Golf.'

Patrick nodded. 'Right, we'll leave him for a minute and check the others. Have you done anything?'

'Tried to stop the bleeding, and splinted an arm on the woman. I'm not a paramedic. I've got a neck splint on the two rear passengers in the jalopy, but otherwise we're stuffed till the fire brigade can cut them out. The old boy looks the worst.'

Anna followed Patrick to the vintage car and peered in. The interior was bathed in blood, and the woman in the back was moaning and crying out. Her legs were trapped by the back of the driver's seat, and it was clear that she was in considerable pain. The man beside her, however, was silent, his face chalky white, and Anna didn't like the look of him at all.

Nor did Patrick. After a quick glance at the driver, to check that he was, indeed, dead, he checked the old man's blood pressure, swore softly, and asked for an intravenous line. Quickly setting up a drip, he squeezed in one unit of Haemacel immediately, changed the bag and handed it to Anna so she could repeat the process while he checked the woman and gave her some pethidine to dull the pain. In the meantime they could hear the other driver, a young man in his early twenties.

'What about me?' he was saying. 'I'm in agony, for God's sake! I need a doctor—oh, God, help me, I'm going to die.'

'I doubt it,' Patrick muttered. 'He's making far too much noise.'

'Do I get the feeling you think it was his fault?' Anna asked softly.

Patrick grinned. 'Did I say that? The fact that this car won't go over thirty-five and he's in a GTi could have nothing to do with it, of course!' He glanced round. 'No seatbelts, you notice. That's why they're so badly injured, because the chassis is good and solid on these old things.'

His patient continued to look grim, despite the forced infusion of Haemacel. Patrick wasn't happy. 'We need to get him out first,' he told the fire brigade. 'Just let us get him stable and then you can start.'

'Right, guv,' the fireman said.

'Take over,' he instructed Anna. 'I'm going to check the other driver. Change the bag over and give him another when it's empty.'

She nodded, and he crossed quickly to the other vehicle. She could hear him speaking, the driver grumbling, Patrick's voice expressionless as he examined him and assured him he would live.

He ordered a spinal splint from the ambulance to be fitted to him because he was complaining of neck pain and tingling fingers, but they were unable to get him out because his lower legs were trapped by the crumpled door pillar.

There was a policeman standing by, and he asked Patrick if he could talk to the man.

'Be my guest,' Patrick said.

As he walked back to Anna, they could hear the policeman's voice.

'Now, sir, I wonder if you could tell me briefly what happened here?'

'What happened? We hit!'

'I see that, sir, the policeman said patiently. 'I wonder if you could tell me how that came to happen?'

'Just because I've got a GTi, I suppose,' the man scoffed.

'No, sir, more because your skid-marks are something in excess of sixty metres in length and you must have still been doing a considerable speed when you hit the other vehicle. Put it down to idle curiosity.'

Patrick smiled grimly at Anna. 'I don't think I'm the only one who's got him tried and convicted. How're our passengers?'

'Weak. His BP's up a little, but not much. This is the fourth unit going in now.'

Patrick whistled softly. 'OK. We've got to get him out.'

He lifted his head and scanned the scene, then waved to the fire brigade officer in charge.

'Over here—we're ready to get this man out now, if you could, please?'

'What about me?' the other driver yelled. 'I'm trapped!'

'Pity it's not by his tongue,' Patrick muttered.

'I think you'll keep a little longer, sunbeam,' the fireman said blithely as he marched past with a portable cutter.

They prised open the front passenger door of the old

car, and the fireman lifted a handbag out of the footwell and put it on the dashboard before trying to tip the seat forward.

Anna stared at the handbag. A horrible suspicion was forming in her mind.

She looked at the elderly lady, still groaning beside her, her handbag clutched like a lifeline in her lap.

'Patrick,' she said quietly, 'I don't want to worry you, but I think there's somebody missing.'

'What?'

He raised his head and looked at the handbag, and then at Anna. 'She might have been flung clear. Ask the woman.'

Anna asked her who was in the car. 'My husband Leslie, my son-in-law Peter and my daughter Lucy,' she whispered. 'How is she? Is she——?' She broke off, clearly distraught, and Anna squeezed her hand.

'I'll find out,' Anna told her. 'I think she was probably flung clear. I'll go and check.'

With a reassuring pat to her shoulder, Anna left her. Because Patrick had given her some pethidine to dull the pain, the woman was drifting in and out of consciousness. Hopefully she would drift out now, and not lie and worry.

Anna ran over to the policeman in charge and told him there was a young woman missing. 'She seems to have been flung clear—she must be in one of the fields or the hedge or something. Can your chaps have a look, please? We need to find her urgently.'

She went back to Patrick and their two patients, and comforted the woman while the dead driver—presumably her son-in-law—was cut free and they started work on freeing her.

Meanwhile her husband was freed and carried carefully away to the waiting ambulance. It went immediately, siren going, and Patrick went too. 'I'll hitch a lift back with it in a minute,' he told Anna as he went, and she nodded.

Good, she wouldn't have to drive that huge car of his. The woman was almost free, and, as Anna supported her arm, they lifted her out on to a waiting stretcher and loaded her into the second ambulance.

Anna stayed, giving her attention to the other driver and worrying about the missing passenger.

'I don't suppose she was just dazed and wandered off?' the police officer suggested worriedly.

Anna shook her head. 'It's possible but—I don't know. Judging by the state of the other occupants, that collision was at quite some speed.'

The policeman nodded. 'I don't suppose a car of that vintage had spectacular brakes, either,' he said. 'If they were bowling along at about thirty, it's quite possible they hadn't slowed down much when they were hit. At that speed she could have been thrown out, I suppose.'

Anna looked around, unable to believe that the woman could have disappeared. She went behind the old car and considered the trajectory she would have followed. Suddenly her eyes focused on the trees just beyond the Golf. Was it possible?

The accident had happened on a bend, so the woman would have been flung clear, over the Golf and——

'There she is!' Anna cried. 'In that tree. Oh, my God, she's hanging upside-down!'

The missing woman was barely visible among the dense foliage in the little stand of trees behind the Golf; she might have gone undetected for weeks so well was she concealed. Only the bright flash of yellow in her scarf had given her away.

Anna started to run, the policeman after her, and when she reached the little stand of field maples she tried to stretch up to the woman.

'Damn, I'm just too short.' She looked around for

something to stand on, and her eye lit on the policeman.

'Give me a leg up,' she said, and, cupping his hands, he made a stirrup for her to use. She hopped lightly up, steadying herself on his head, and quickly felt for pulse in the woman's neck.

'She's alive,' Anna called down. 'I need to get up to her. Give me a boost up the tree, and get the fire brigade over here fast. We need to work out a way of getting her down without injuring her any further.'

Employing the services of the police officer yet again, Anna scrambled up the tree and wriggled out along another branch that brought her up beside the woman.

It was only then that the scale of her injuries began to be apparent.

'Her right leg—the one that's caught—is broken where it's trapped. Fortunately her jeans seem to be taking most of the strain. Her left arm looks a little strange—it's hanging as if she's dislocated her shoulder, I think. And she could well have a spinal injury,' Anna called down to the fire officer. 'How do you suggest getting her down?'

'Carefully,' the man said. 'I'll call a vehicle with a lift on the rear——'

'We haven't got time. She's been here too long as it is, I'm worried about this foot. No, I'll have to tie her other leg to this one as a splint, tie a rope to her knees and sling it over a higher branch, and then we'll have to lower her down. She'll need a spinal splint on when she's low enough, before you start to lift her down, because if she's had a back injury we're going to have to be very careful.'

'Right.' The fire officer turned, shouted instructions, and seconds later another man started to climb the little tree.

It creaked ominously, and Anna yelled at him. 'It

won't take all of us. Just let me do it, OK? Pass me the stuff.'

'Know your knots, do you, gal?' the fireman asked with a grin.

'I used to be a Girl Guide. Chuck me the rope.'

It took only a few minutes, but to Anna they seemed agonising.

Just when she was stretched out at arm's length, her legs wrapped round the branch, tightening the last knot, the ambulance came back with Patrick.

'Oh, hell,' she muttered, knowing what he would say.

She was right.

'Anna, for God's sake!' he called, striding towards her. 'What on earth are you doing? Hold on to something!'

'I am—my temper. This is hard enough. OK, try that—great. Now lift slowly—pull—that's it—STOP!'

She freed the damaged foot from the fork in the branch that had supported her, lashed it lightly to the other foot and to the rope, and then the firemen lowered her to the ground, paying out the rope as they went.

The ambulance crew fitted a spinal splint, lowered her carefully on to a stretcher, and then Patrick was standing over her, checking her rapidly.

'She seems remarkably stable,' he said as Anna slithered to the ground and crossed over to them. 'That foot looks grim, and her shoulder's dislocated—better radio in and have an orthopod at the ready. Otherwise she seems remarkably well. Her pupils are reacting, but she's probably slightly concussed. Who spotted her?'

'I did,' Anna told him, and he grinned.

'Now, why didn't I guess?'

They watched her go, the siren wailing, and Patrick

then turned to Anna. 'I can't trust you for a second, can I?' he complained gently, and tugged her into his arms. 'Well done. Brave girl. That was a very well-managed descent, on the patient's part at least.' He held her at arm's length and studied her. 'Tell me,' he murmured, 'how are you going to explain the destruction of yet another uniform dress?'

Anna laughed, warmed to the marrow by his praise. 'I do seem to be getting through them, don't I?'

He hugged her again briefly, then turned back to the police officer, who was eyeing them with mild curiosity. 'Is our boy racer nearly free yet?'

The policeman nodded his head. 'Almost. They're just taking the bulkhead to bits now.'

'I'd better go and show a little compassion,' he said with a grim smile, and Anna followed him over to the car.

'Hang on, we'll give him some pethidine before you do that. He's been stuck a good while, it's bound to be painful.'

'At bloody last—some medical attention,' the man grumbled petulantly.

'I'm sorry,' Patrick told him, 'we've been rather busy—the other casualties were worse off than you by some considerable margin.'

'How, worse off?' he asked grumpily. 'Can't see a damn thing from here, with the windscreen shattered.'

Patrick hesitated. 'The other driver died. The three passengers have all sustained serious injuries. One of them may not make it.'

The man went pale, and swore softly under his breath. 'I never realised it was that bad,' he told them. 'They came flying round that corner—hell, they weren't even looking! They were talking and laughing—the driver had his head turned, poor bastard. Are they all gone to hospital now?'

Patrick nodded, suddenly wondering if he had mis-judged the man. 'Yes, they've all gone now. Let's get you out and see how your legs are.'

'They're fine,' he said, clearly subdued. 'I can move them, anyway. The painkiller's helped.'

The firemen cut away the last section of bulkhead with the pneumatic jaws, and lifted the offending slab of metal away from his legs.

Then, by sliding the seat back as far as it would go, they were able to lift him out and put him on a stretcher and load him into the last ambulance that was waiting.

They saw it off, then trudged back to Patrick's car with their equipment.

'I don't suppose we'll ever know the truth,' Anna said thoughtfully.

'The truth? The guy in the GTi was going too fast, you can tell that by his skidmarks, but it sounds as if he wasn't the only one at fault. As you say, we may never know.'

They reached the car and Anna eyed the cream leather upholstery doubtfully. 'I don't like to sit in your father's car like this,' she said with a disparaging glance at her bloodstained and green-streaked clothes.

Patrick's mouth tilted in a wry smile. 'It doesn't matter—my father doesn't think it's his.'

'Even so,' she said, and, shaking out a sterile drape, she spread it over the seat before she got in.

'Fussbudget,' he told her, but she knew she was right.

'Just because your father's too ill now to remember his car doesn't mean I should treat it with any less care than he would have done,' she told Patrick quietly.

She saw respect dawn in his eyes, and something else—something that, if she were an optimistic fool, she might call love.

Then he turned away and started the car. 'Come on,

'we must get back,' he said, and she wasn't sure if it was her imagination or if his voice had, indeed, sounded just a little gruff. . .

By the time they got back to the hospital the girl Anna had rescued from the tree had regained consciousness and was talking. The police were anxious to interview her, but the orthopaedic surgeon informed them bluntly that they could wait until after she had had surgery to reduce the fractures in her lower leg.

Apparently she was asking for her husband, and Anna wondered how she would feel when she learned he was dead.

How would she feel if it was Patrick?

She glanced at his face as Tim Mayhew, the orthopaedic consultant, asked if he should tell her about her husband or if Patrick would do it.

She saw the strain around Patrick's eyes, and remembered that he had lost his wife suddenly in a tragic accident. How had he felt?

'I'll tell her,' he said quietly, and Anna had a sudden inkling of what it would cost him to do so. She went with him, as much to support him as to support the woman.

She was in a cubicle on a trolley, and Patrick went in and took her hand. 'Lucy?' he said softly.

She turned towards him, her eyes huge in her pale face.

'How's Peter? I want to see him.'

Patrick was silent for a moment, then Anna saw his thumb stroking the back of her hand in a silent gesture of comfort.

'Lucy, I'm sorry, there was nothing we could do to save him. He died instantly.'

Her face went even paler, her eyes widening. 'No! No, you're lying to me!'

Patrick's face contracted. 'I wish I were. I'm so sorry.'

She lay for a minute, absorbing the information, then her eyes fluttered shut. 'What did he die of?' she asked faintly.

'We don't know yet. There'll be a post mortem — that will tell us. Probably a ruptured aorta — and that's about as instant as it can be. He would have felt nothing.'

A deep shudder ran through her, and Patrick held her hand between his and talked to her gently until the shudders gave way to sobs, then he turned to Anna.

His face was chalk-white and deep lines were etched in it.

'Stay with her,' he said gruffly, and, turning on his heel, he strode out. Anna could only guess at the pain he was suffering — probably suffered every time he had to perform this dismal task.

The porter came to take Lucy to Theatre, and Anna went with her, holding her hand all the way. By the time they arrived she was calmer, although still very shocked.

'I'll give her a light anaesthetic. They aren't going to plate the leg,' the anaesthetist said. 'I don't want to send her too deep when she's in shock.'

Anna handed Lucy over to him and went back down to A and E. It was already after four, and after taking one look at her Kathleen sent her home.

'I owe you one — at least!' she said. 'I would have killed you if I'd known what you were doing, but I can't tell you how grateful I am that you talked to him.'

Anna smiled tiredly. 'My pleasure. It's a good job I know he isn't violent. He was pretty mad with me.'

Kath laughed. 'Oh, he yells a bit. I usually ignore him and he settles down after a while!' She sobered and laid her hand on Anna's shoulder. 'Thanks, anyway. I'm very grateful. Now go home.'

Anna paused. 'Tell Patrick I've gone, will you? I can't find him.'

'Jack sent him off. He looked pretty grim. I'm going off now, too. I'll see you on Tuesday.'

Anna went home, wondering if she should phone Patrick and see if he was all right. She didn't, though, because she sensed that he needed the space. He would come to her if he wanted to talk.

He did come, but not to talk. The doorbell rang at about nine-thirty, and when she opened it he came in, a faint smile of greeting on his face. It didn't hide his mood, though.

'Are you OK?' she asked softly, reaching up to cup his face.

He heaved a deep breath and let it out in a whoosh. 'Yes, I'm OK.'

'Was it talking to Lucy?'

He nodded, but said nothing more. She put her arms round him, and then his head descended, taking her mouth in a hungry kiss that clamoured for more.

Without preamble she led him upstairs, and his lovemaking was wild and desperate, a passionate declaration of the life-force inside him.

Afterwards he was silent, holding her, and yet, she sensed, not there at all.

She had never felt his wife's presence so acutely.

CHAPTER EIGHT

ANNA didn't expect to see him until Monday, when they were both on duty, but the doorbell rang on Saturday morning at nine.

She was still in her dressing-gown after a sleepless night spent agonising over her love for him, and when she opened the door she was astonished to see him.

'Patrick!' she exclaimed. 'Is everything all right?'

He gave her a box of chocolates and a wry smile.

'Sorry,' he said. 'I was in a pretty grim mood last night. When I got home my mother was upset about my father, the agency nurse had gone home for the weekend and she was wondering if she'd done the right thing. By the time I got away I was feeling pretty uptight. I wasn't the best company.'

It didn't quite ring true, but Anna accepted the smile, the apology and the chocolates with good grace.

'Are you coming in?'

'What about Flissy?'

'What about her? She'd love to see you again.'

He gave her an odd look. 'Don't you mind?'

Her smile was rueful. 'Patrick, you've already stolen her heart.'

And mine, she could have added, but didn't.

His face softened in a tender smile as Flissy appeared round Anna's legs.

He crouched down and she ran into his arms without hesitation. 'Hello, Patrick!' she squealed, and he lifted her up in his arms and hugged her.

'Hello, Tuppence. How are you?'

'Fine. Mummy took my stitches out—want to see?'

She showed him her hand, and Patrick duly admired it and kissed it, this time on the little scar itself.

She giggled. 'That tickles,' she told him.

'It does?' He opened her fingers again and blew a raspberry in the palm of her hand, which had her in squeals of wriggly laughter. With a smile he set her down and looked at Anna. 'Are you busy?'

'Today?'

He nodded, and she felt the awful unhappiness of the night fade away under his tender gaze. Could he look at her like that if he still loved his wife? Of course he had sad memories. She would have to live with that, as he did. That didn't mean they could have no future, surely?

'No, we're not busy,' she told him. 'Fliss has ballet at the music school at ten, but otherwise we're free.'

'Have you got your car back yet?'

She shook her head. 'No. Maybe once I've been paid I can afford to get it fixed.'

He hesitated, then made a suggestion. 'You know the agency nurse is off this weekend and we're on our own? How about if you and Flissy come over for the weekend, help with my father, and instead of paying you I'll get your car fixed. Would that seem reasonable?'

It sounded terribly tempting. Flissy would have a wonderful time, and with Patrick around Anna was sure she would, too. However, her car repair would be expensive.

'That sounds a bit of a raw deal,' she told him. 'The car's not going to be cheap to fix.'

He grinned. 'Nor is my mother's nervous break-down. And I shouldn't worry, the agency nurse is far from cheap. If you feel you're ripping us off, you can always do another weekend, or am I just being selfish wanting you all weekend as well as during the week?'

Anna couldn't think of anything she'd prefer. However, she wasn't the only one to consider. 'What does your mother think?' she asked.

'I have no idea—I've only just thought of it. I'll go and discuss it with her now, and you take Fliss to ballet. I'll pick you up from there, bring you back, and we can collect your things—OK?'

She nodded, overtaken by events and a little bemused. The whole weekend with him?

It sounded like a little slice of paradise.

Anna was standing in the corridor outside the ballet class when she became aware of Patrick's presence. She turned, and across the crowd of waiting parents their eyes locked.

He made his way through to her, hopefully oblivious to her thrashing heart, and winked. 'OK?'

She nodded. 'What did your mother say?'

'She was delighted. She's really looking forward to having Flissy for the weekend, and all her panics about looking after my father are laid to rest. She says I'm to tell you you're a treasure.'

Anna laughed a little uncomfortably. 'Nonsense.'

'Uh-uh! Treasures don't argue,' he told her firmly.

'Then it just goes to prove I'm not one,' she quipped back, enjoying the warmth around her heart.

He bent forward and peered through the glass at the top of the door.

'Is Flissy in there?'

'Yes—in pink.'

'They're all in pink.'

'Quite.'

He chuckled, then went still, his face creasing in a tender smile. 'I can see her,' he said softly, and Anna watched him, fascinated, as he watched Flissy.

Anybody would think he really cared about her,

Anna thought, and the need for that to be true was like a pain in her heart. If only it could be.

'I think they've finished,' he said, and then the door opened and lots of tiny little pink-clad children came out, eyes sparkling.

Flissy danced up to them. 'Hello. Are we going?'

Anna nodded. 'Yes, we are.'

'Oh, yippee! Come on!'

She grabbed Anna and Patrick by the hands and started to tow them towards the stairs, her excitement almost tangible.

They didn't change her, because Patrick said his mother would love to see her in her ballet clothes, so they went back to Mulberry Terrace, picked up their few things, and went back to the house.

Maggie greeted them at the door, making a huge fuss of Flissy and exclaiming over how lovely she looked.

'George, see, isn't she beautiful?'

Anna followed them in, and saw a stooped, grey-haired man in a wheelchair in the kitchen lift his head and smile with Patrick's smile.

'Well, what a delightful little minx! Hello, my dear. Who are you?'

'I'm Flissy,' she told him. 'Why are you in a wheelchair?'

He pulled a face. 'My legs don't seem to be too good these days.'

Anna walked up behind Flissy and held out her hand. 'Hello. I'm Anna Jarvis, Flissy's mother. I'm sorry about her lack of tact.'

He laughed. 'Oh, my dear, don't apologise. It's quite refreshing. Have we had breakfast?'

'Yes, darling,' Maggie said patiently. 'Are you hungry? Would you like a cup of coffee? I was just going to make one for Anna and Patrick.'

George Haddon's head swivelled and he looked up at Patrick. 'You here again, young man? Very kind of you, I'm sure.'

Patrick's smile tore Anna's heart.

'It's my pleasure,' he said softly, and looked across at his mother. 'Thanks, we'd love a coffee. Can I help you?'

'No, dear, take your father in the garden. It's such a lovely day, but I can't get the wheelchair over the step.'

'No problem.'

Patrick flicked off the brakes with his foot, turned the chair round and wheeled his father out, Flissy dancing along behind him. As they went Anna could hear George saying, 'She will keep calling me your father. Strange woman, my wife—gets a bit muddled about things. We had a son once, you know. He was called Patrick, but he'd be younger than you—about twenty, I think. That must be what's confusing her.'

Anna met Maggie's eyes and they shared a sad smile.

'Poor Patrick. He really can't bear it. We're both so glad you could come for the weekend—not just because you're a nurse, but because Flissy will take his mind off his father and he'll get a break from the endless denial. It really hurts him so badly.'

She poured the water on the instant coffee and set the kettle down with a sigh. 'He does understand,' she continued, 'but I don't think it makes it any easier. And George will keep repeating himself until we could all scream. I think he must have asked me ten times if we've had breakfast. Then it will be lunch, or the time, or the day, or are we going to church—it never stops——'

She broke off, her composure rattled, and Anna waited, saying nothing, as she gathered herself together again.

'I'm sorry,' she sighed. 'It just gets so hard sometimes.'

'I think it's wonderful of you to have him at home,' Anna said. 'It can't be easy, either emotionally or physically. Patrick told me he's incontinent.'

She nodded. 'Yes. Patrick deals with that, though. He says he doesn't mind, and I suppose he's had plenty of practice. It's a good job we'd still got the wheelchair.'

Anna was puzzled. 'Wheelchair?' she asked. 'Practice?'

'With Isobel.'

Anna stared at Maggie. 'Isobel?' she said incredulously.

'Oh, yes—didn't you know? She had spina bifida— she was in a wheelchair most of the time. She could walk a little at first, but then she had a nasty fall down the stairs and lost the little feeling she had left. After that Patrick had to do almost everything for her care.' Maggie looked at her curiously. 'Didn't he tell you?'

Anna shook her head. 'No. No, he's told me almost nothing about her.'

'Oh, well, I'm sorry. I don't suppose it was a secret. Let's go out and join them, shall we?'

Anna felt too shocked to face him. 'I'll be out in a minute—I just want to go to the loo,' she told Maggie, and going into the cloakroom, she pulled the door shut and leaned back on it. Isobel had had spina bifida? She had been paraplegic? Why hadn't he told her?

She washed her face and hands, staring at herself in the mirror for a moment as she dried her face. Did the shock still show? Not really, she decided.

She put the towel back and went out into the garden. George was sitting in the shade of a birch tree with his wife, and Patrick and Flissy were talking to the pony.

Flissy turned and saw her, then beckoned her over. 'Mummy, he's lovely. Come and pat him,' she called.

Anna went, unable to meet Patrick's eye, and Flissy turned her little face up to her mother. 'Can I ride him? Please, please?'

'Maybe later,' Patrick said, searching Anna's face. 'We've got a cup of coffee going cold. You're here for the weekend; I'm sure there'll be plenty of opportunities for you to sit on him.'

Anna held out her hand, and Flissy took it reluctantly, trailing back over the lawn behind them.

Maggie called her as they approached. 'Flissy, the kittens are about somewhere. They might be sleeping by the Aga in the kitchen, in their box. Want to go and see?'

She held out her hand, and Flissy went eagerly. Anna tensed, her buffer gone, and sat down on the chair Patrick held for her. His father had dozed off, and there was nothing between her and Patrick but silence.

He broke it gently.

'What's wrong?'

She might have realised she couldn't get anything past him. 'Your mother just told me about Isobel and her spina bifida,' she said, and even to her ears her voice sounded strained.

'Oh. I'm sorry, I never thought to mention it. It wasn't relevant.'

Anna turned to him. 'Not relevant? How can you say that?'

He gave a short laugh. 'Well, it never was to her. I married a woman, Anna, not a cripple. Her disability was a long way down her list of vital statistics. If you'd met her you would have realised that. She made no allowances for herself at all. Hell, the first year we were married she even walked to the top of Ben Nevis.

She screamed blue murder when I carried her down.'
He grunted. 'That was before her accident on the
stairs. After that she had to be more sensible. Even
Isobel realised that.'

Anna fiddled with the spoon in her coffee. 'You
never talk about her.'

His face closed. 'You want me to?'

She shrugged. 'She was a large part of your life.'

He gave his attention to a biscuit, crumbling it
unheeded into his lap. 'Yes.' He stood up abruptly,
scattering crumbs all over the grass, and held out his
hand to her. 'Come with me.'

She took his hand, not surprised at the tension in it,
and followed him towards a door into a wing by the
side of the house. A huge lilac bush grew by the wall,
its blooms now faded, and Anna realised that this must
be the converted stable flat where he lived.

She went through the door after him and found
herself in a large, cool room overlooking the garden. It
was simply but comfortably furnished, and she could
see a bedroom through a door at the far side. He led
her through it, and there beside the big bed was a
photograph in a plain silver frame of a laughing girl
with flying hair, racing a wheelchair over a finishing
line.

He handed it to her. 'That was Isobel after her
accident. She did the London Marathon.'

Anna was humbled in the face of such determination.
Staring at the girl, her lovely face etched with strain
but victorious, she felt a lump in her throat. She handed
the photo back.

'She was very lovely.'

Patrick stared at the photo, his face expressionless.

'Yes. Yes, she was.' He set it down with exaggerated
care, and then met Anna's eyes. 'We had a real
marriage,' he told her, almost as if he was warning her

not to dismiss Isobel just because she had been crippled. 'We shared everything. It's important that you realise that. She was, in every sense, a real wife.'

Anna blushed and turned away from the harshness of his voice, ashamed of the tiny spurt of hope she had felt when she had realised Isobel was crippled—the hope that perhaps Patrick had never made love to her as he did to Anna.

Jealousy of a dead woman was a terrible thing. She dashed the tears from her cheeks, and Patrick's hand was gentle on her shoulder.

'I'm sorry, Anna,' he said softly. 'You had to know that. I didn't want you thinking we had less of a marriage than we did.'

He left her then, walking quietly out, and Anna turned and looked at the photo of the dead girl. Her laughing eyes seemed to challenge Anna, and she felt a strange peace steal over her.

There was a voice in her head, distant but very determined. Fight for him. For God's sake, don't let him go on like this. If you don't fight, you don't deserve him.

She touched the picture, her fingers tracing the face with gentle reverence. 'I'll do my best,' she vowed. 'I love him. I won't hurt him—that, at least, I can promise you.'

Suddenly cold, she turned and left the room without a backward glance.

George Haddon was a dear man, Anna decided later that day. He seemed surprised that she was a nurse, but once she had washed him and got him to bed he acknowledged that she seemed to know what she was doing.

'Is that little thing your daughter?' he asked, for what seemed like the hundreth time that day.

'Yes, she is,' Anna told him with a smile.

'Delightful child. We had a son once, you know. Used to ride that pony that your daughter's taken such a liking to. He was quite good at it—did all sorts of pony club shows and things. Used to worry me. Did Margaret tell you I was an orthopaedic surgeon? I saw some rum old injuries from riding accidents.'

He noticed Anna's worried look, and patted her hand. 'Oh, my dear, I didn't mean to worry you. Toby's all right. It's these great big eventers that are so dangerous. Too brave for their own good. They hurl themselves in where angels fear to tread.'

Anna could sympathise. She was doing exactly that with Patrick, she realised. She settled George comfortably and handed him his book, making sure his bell was in reach. 'Just call me if you need me,' she told him. 'I'm going to put Flissy to bed now.'

'Strange names people give their children these days,' he said with a smile, so once again Anna explained the origin of her daughter's nickname.

George chuckled. 'Dear little thing—you say she's your daughter? Or that young man who says he's my son?'

'No,' she said patiently. 'Flissy's mine.'

'And you aren't married to Patrick?'

'No.'

He grunted. 'Should be. Way he's been watching you all day, it's a wonder your clothes haven't caught fire. Now, what do you say this bell is for?'

'If you need me,' Anna said again, and with a gentle smile she left the room and pulled the door to.

Patrick was standing outside, and had clearly been listening.

'Relentless, isn't it?' he said heavily.

'He's a dear,' Anna defended kindly. 'He's been

really sweet with Flissy. I think he must have been a very wonderful father.'

Patrick swallowed and turned away, but not before she saw the pain in his eyes. 'He was. He taught me how to fish, and we used to go crabbing at Orford when I was—oh, tiny. Flissy's age.' He turned back, his emotions under control again. 'We ought to take her crabbing; she'd love it.'

Anna laughed. 'She'd fall in.'

'Nonsense. She's got natural balance. You're much more likely to fall in,' he teased, but Anna couldn't laugh.

It was too true. The way he kept her permanently off-balance, it was a wonder she could walk straight!

'What are you doing now?' he asked.

'Putting Flissy to bed.'

'Can I help?'

She stared at him in surprise. 'Sure. You really want to?'

'Uh-huh. She's gorgeous.'

She realised then with a shock that Patrick would have loved children, still longed for them. She should have seen it before, but now it really hit her. Not only did Flissy adore Patrick, but Patrick too had fallen for Flissy.

If she couldn't get through to him, then how much pain would they all feel?

She shivered at the thought, and Patrick put an arm round her. 'Cold?' he asked solicitously.

'Mmm—a little,' she lied. 'I'll get a cardigan in a minute.'

They found Flissy in the kitchen, curled up with the kittens, all of them fast asleep.

'Leave her for a minute. Come and have a drink, you look bushed,' Maggie said. 'George is a dear but he can be very wearing, and you've been at work all week. You really should be having a rest.'

'But I've done practically nothing all day,' Anna argued gently. 'I feel such a fraud. You must let me do more.'

Maggie smiled. 'Perhaps tomorrow. Now, come and have a drink. What would you like? Gin and tonic? Wine? Sherry? Whisky? Martini?'

'Oh—white wine if it's open, please, but don't open one just for me.'

'I wouldn't dream of it,' Patrick teased, taking a bottle out of the fridge and pulling the cork with practised ease. He poured two glasses, handed her one and turned to his mother. 'What can I get you?'

'A little gin and tonic, I think, dear, please. Shall we take it in the conservatory?'

They sat and gazed across the garden, and Maggie sighed. 'It's looking so wild. George is really upset about it.'

Anna had an idea. 'There's very little to do for him,' she said. 'Could I spend some time on the flower-beds tomorrow? Would he let me?'

Maggie lookd doubtful. 'Do you know what you're doing?' she asked.

Anna gave a short, humourless laugh. 'Oh, yes. My grandmother made sure I knew which plants to pull up, and the Latin names of those I shouldn't. Don't worry, I know what I'm doing, and it's such a pretty garden it would be a pleasure. I've missed having a real garden to work on. Anyway, if you're worried, I could always park his wheelchair beside me and we could do it together. He could talk me through it—it would give him a purpose. He hates being so useless.'

Maggie thought it was a wonderful idea, so in the morning, after Anna had bathed and dressed Flissy and George, they went in the garden.

Starting at one end, Anna talked about the plants, using their Latin names so that George knew she wasn't completely ignorant, but deferring enough to him that he didn't feel redundant.

After a while the tension in her shoulders eased, and she was able to forget about her troubles with Patrick and just take pleasure in the day and the simple tasks it had brought. Patrick put Flissy on Toby again, this time with his saddle and bridle, and they went for a walk up the bridleway beside the house while Anna tried not to be a worrywart and concentrated on the plants.

It was a plantsman's paradise, although George could no longer remember all the Latin names, and Anna had a wonderful time.

'They'll need splitting this autumn,' George said thoughtfully. 'That *alchemilla mollis* is getting ridiculous, and the little *iris reticulata* in behind it is almost lost. It would be better over there by the white geranium, but it can't be moved now. The *pulmonaria* is getting out of control, as well—oh, damn, I feel so helpless. . .'

Tears of frustration formed in his eyes, and Anna held his hand and smiled. 'Then you need help. I can move them for you in the autumn.'

He studied her. 'Are you sure you don't mind? I seem to be taking advantage of your good nature over and over again.'

Anna, who was more than conscious of the fact that she was being paid for doing something she enjoyed, shook her head. 'No, honestly. I don't have a garden any more, and I would love to be able to help you here. I've missed it.'

She realised she had, although her feelings for gardening were so inextricably linked with her feelings for her grandmother that it was hard to separate the two.

Today, though, working in the cool damp soil with Patrick's father by her side, her sense of perspective began to return. She even found a small measure of forgiveness in her heart. Her grandmother, after all, had been brought up in much stricter times, when nice girls didn't do what Anna had done.

Anna admitted that 'nice' girls probably still didn't, and was able to forgive her grandmother her harsh judgement, although she knew she wasn't a whore, just a foolish girl who had made a terrible mistake and had had to pay the price.

Flissy arrived back just then on Toby, and as Anna looked at her she wondered if paying the price hadn't been the most wonderful gift of all.

Bringing her up wasn't easy, either financially or emotionally. Other people, even in this day and age, still distanced themselves from her, and most of Flissy's friends had only one parent. It was as though the married parents were afraid that Flissy's illegitimacy would rub off, she thought wryly.

Even so, despite all their problems, Anna couldn't imagine life without her little treasure. No, the positive certainly outweighed the negative.

Getting to her feet, she tugged off her gloves and smiled at George. 'Shall I put you back in the shade for a while? It's a bit hot here, I don't want you getting heatstroke.'

She wheeled him back to the birch tree and locked the wheels, then, brushing her hands against her jeans, she strolled over to the paddock. 'Hi.'

'Hi—Mummy, we saw a deer!' Flissy exclaimed, bubbling over, and Patrick lifted her down and she wriggled back under the fence and told Anna all about it, her voice getting higher and higher with excitement.

Anna looked at Patrick over her head. 'What fun. Do you often see them?'

He shook his head. 'No, not really. Sometimes they stray out of the woods, but not often. It must have come to see Flissy.'

He gave Flissy a smile of such tenderness that Anna's heart ached. If only he would look at her like that. . .

She pulled herself up short. What was she thinking about, being jealous of her four-year-old-daughter? Ashamed, she took Flissy's hand. 'I expect you're thirsty after all that excitement. Shall we go and find you a drink and make Patrick and Mr Haddon a cup of coffee?'

Flissy nodded, curls bouncing. 'Can I have a biscuit, too?'

'I expect so.'

She flashed a brief smile at Patrick. 'Come and join us when you're ready,' she told him, and then, with Flissy prancing on her arm, Anna went over to the house and into the cool, quiet kitchen, away from Patrick and her endless, tumbling emotions.

He joined them there a few minutes later, taking the tray for her, and Flissy climbed on George's lap and told him all about the deer.

'Well, how exciting,' he said, his eyes wide with pretended astonishment.

'It was,' Flissy assured him, and slipped off his lap, running over to Toby to give him a piece of biscuit.

'What a dear little girl,' George said indulgently.

'She is,' Patrick said, watching Flissy with Toby. 'She's a delight. She's very easy to love.'

He looked at Anna, and she could have wept, because his eyes were sad. It was as if he was apologising because he couldn't love her, only her daughter.

She felt helpless. It was easy for Isobel to throw down challenges, she thought irrationally, but she wasn't Isobel. She wasn't a fighter—never had been, never would be. If things got too much she retreated, avoiding them.

Perhaps that was why she allowed her relationship with Patrick to drift, instead of pushing for more of a commitment.

He never said he was coming round, just turned up when he felt like it, so she never knew whether to expect him or not.

It wasn't that he was inconsiderate, just that he was keeping their relationship casual.

His lovemaking, though, was far from casual. It was as if that was the only time he could be himself, without reserve, and Anna was sure he couldn't be so tender and loving if he felt nothing.

So why the hiding from commitment?

Unless, like her, he was avoiding the issue. Perhaps he was afraid of rejection, or maybe he was trying to fight the attraction.

Perhaps he almost resented his need for her, because of his love for Isobel. Anna didn't know. The only sure thing in her world was that if she didn't win his love, her life stretched ahead of her like a barren wasteland.

No, she thought, not quite barren.

She had Flissy.

Patrick had nothing. . .

CHAPTER NINE

THEY were on duty together on the Bank Holiday Monday, the day after Anna's weekend at the Haddons' house with Flissy.

It was another glorious day of hot sun, bright skies and sporting accidents.

Patrick had taken Anna and Flissy home the night before on his way into the hospital to take over from Jack Lawrence, who had been on duty for the weekend.

When Anna arrived on Monday morning, it was to find that Patrick had already been in the department since four.

'Nasty RTA,' he told her. 'No one dead, but it wasn't for want of trying. Oh, by the way, the old boy in the vintage car on Friday died.'

Anna sighed. Poor Lucy, she thought, losing her husband and her father in one accident. She wondered how she was coping, but didn't feel she could intrude. She would have plenty of visitors, Anna was sure.

The morning casualties started to trickle in, and, it being a bank holiday, they were the usual.

One man came in almost totally devoid of skin on his back. He had been sailing the day before and had gone to bed with sunburn, only to wake up in the night and find his skin had blistered and stuck to the sheet. When he tried to get up, he had left it all behind. In addition to his pain and skin damage, he was suffering from a high temperature and all the symptoms of heatstroke.

Patrick admitted him, grumbling gently about the

153

waste of health service resources when people couldn't exercise a little common sense, and turned his attention next to a man who had mashed his finger in the tow hitch of his caravan.

'I couldn't get it on,' he said, 'so I jumped on the hitch, just as my finger slipped.'

It was broken, messy and painful, but there was no serious damage and Anna strapped it up for him and sent him on his way with the suggestion that he buy a bit of grease for the workings.

'I will,' he said in a heartfelt voice, and Anna shook her head.

The fine weather brought them all out, she thought wryly.

Then there was a call from Ambulance Control. A young woman was being brought in from a horse show. Her horse had somersaulted over a jump and landed on her, and she had suspected back and pelvic injuries, and possibly a ruptured spleen.

They cleared Crash, dealt with the patients who were already under way, and then the sound of the siren filtered into the department.

'We're on,' Patrick said, and together they went to the entrance to wait for their patient.

She was unloaded with great care, and as they wheeled her in Anna could tell she was furious.

'I can't believe I was so stupid,' she was saying. 'I should have rolled out of the way! I knew he was going to do it. Ouch!'

Patrick gave her a wry grin. 'It's easy to be wise after the event. Can we have your name, please?'

'Helen Morgan,' she said through gritted teeth. 'If I've broken my bloody pelvis again I'm going to scream.'

'You've done it before?' Patrick asked.

She snorted. 'Oh, yes. This place and I are old

friends. I did it last April. Is Nick Davidson around? I'd like him to fix me if possible.'

Patrick laughed softly. 'Let's just see if it's necessary first, can we? Where do you hurt?'

Her reply was rude and to the point.

'OK,' Patrick said, making no attempt to hide his smile. 'We'll check you over, X-ray you, and see where we go from there. Anna, could we cut those jodhpurs off, please?'

'No!' Helen yelled. 'They're brand-new. Don't you dare cut them off!'

Anna stared at her. 'But your pelvis is probably broken, and you might have a spinal injury. I can't pull them off.'

'Pull them off or I'll do it,' the woman threatened. Looking at her, Anna had no doubt she meant it.

With a shrug, she eased the jodhpurs down as carefully as she could, pausing when Helen winced and swore.

'Go on,' she said impatiently, so Anna finished the job as carefully as she could.

Patrick stood back and looked at the position of her legs, both of them fallen out to the side, and the swelling and bruising which was appearing over the pubic bone and under the pubic arch.

He looked at her; she looked back at him and she sighed heavily. 'I've done it again, haven't I? Same horse, same damn fence—it's time he was cat food.'

It was quite clear that she didn't mean it, but personally Anna felt there was some considerable truth in Helen's words.

Patrick carefully slid his hand into the small of her back, palm upwards, and felt for any spinal abnormalities. 'Well, I can't feel anything, but you'll need some photos of that spine too, just to be on the safe side.

We'll get you X-rayed and get Nick down here—his firm's on take today.'

'Thank God for that. I don't want anyone else mucking about with me. Hell, that is sore.'

Anna checked her blood pressure, which was good, and Patrick gave her a shot of pethidine to dull the pain and put in an IV line, taking blood for cross-matching. Judging by the amount of bruising that was already coming out, she was bleeding heavily into the fractures and would probably need transfusing. It seemed unlikely, though, that she had sustained any internal injuries.

'I wonder if we shouldn't get a gynaecologist to take a look at you?' Patrick suggested quietly as he studied her bruising. 'Your pelvic floor seems to have taken a bit of a battering.'

'There's no way anyone's rummaging around in there,' Helen said candidly. 'It's too damned sore. They can wait till I'm unconscious.'

Patrick nodded. 'Good idea. Right, let's get these plates and go from there.'

The damage was restricted to her pelvis, the plates revealed. That was the good news. The bad news was that the plate Nick had put in last year had buckled and broken free, and had reopened the old fracture as well.

Nick, when he was called down, eyed Helen with despair. 'Not you again,' he groaned. 'Look at it! Not content with mashing yourself up again, you've got to go and mess up the last lot!'

He tugged the plates down after studying them, and pushed the spinal ones up into the clips on the light-box.

'No spinal damage, thank goodness, and your ribs and other bits look OK. Right.'

He pulled the spinal plates down, put the first ones back up and sighed.

'Just what I needed—forty-eight hours in Theatre with you.'

She snorted. 'Last time it was six.'

'Last time was easy,' he retorted. He bent over her and studied the bruising, and sighed. 'Helen, you've really messed yourself up this time. I think the chances of being able to put you back together so you can have children normally are very slight.'

She shrugged. 'I've got two. Why would I want any more? So long as I can sit on a horse, that'll do me.'

Anna closed her eyes in disbelief. And Kathleen was worried about Jack being irresponsible!

'I'll get a gynae doctor to look at you while you're in Theatre. We may have to work together on this repair.'

She rolled her eyes. 'What an idiot,' she said again, and Anna saw her eyes fill. 'Can somebody ring my husband, please? He's at home with the children. He won't watch me compete.'

'I wonder why?' Patrick said under his breath.

'Oh, don't,' she sighed. 'I know I've been a fool. I shouldn't have pushed him, he was all set up wrong— probably remembered his fall there last year. All I could think was, I had to get him over. Still, good job I had my body protector on or it might have been even worse.'

Anna, eyeing the X-rays, could well believe it. 'Give me your husband's number,' she said gently, 'and I'll ring him now.'

'Oh, thanks.' She dictated the number, then said, 'Could you also ring another number? It's the livery stable near me. I want them to collect Shamus from the showground and look after him.'

She phoned Mr Morgan first, to find that he was on

the way, having called a neighbour in to look after the children. When he arrived Anna intercepted him.

'How is she?' he asked immediately. He looked harassed and worried to death.

Anna felt sorry for him. 'She's not too bad. She's fractured her pelvis again, though. The doctor would like to see you—he can tell you more. In the meantime could you sign the consent form for her operation? She'll need to have it fixed again.'

His shoulders drooped. 'Crazy woman. Still, it's over now. Don't tell her, for God's sake, but they had to shoot the horse.'

'Oh, dear,' Anna said automatically, but she didn't really mean it.

'It's a relief,' the man told her. 'He had more courage than sense, and Helen just doesn't seem to know when to be afraid.'

Anna smiled at him. 'I think she's afraid now—afraid and very cross with herself. I'm sure she'd be very pleased to see you.'

'Hmm. She'll be even more cross with herself when she knows the horse is dead. Oh, well. . .'

Anna took him into the cubicle, and, after a tearful greeting from his wife, Patrick led him aside and showed him the X-ray plates.

He swore softly. 'She's really done a number this time,' he said, studying them. 'There'll be gynae implications as well, I expect—her uterus looks displaced, and this bit here——' he indicated a sharp end of bone pointing inwards '—is going to interfere with her bladder unless it's shifted.'

'Are you a doctor?' Patrick asked in surprise.

'No—I'm a vet, but the principle's the same. Hell.'

Anna interrupted them. 'The porter's here to take Helen up to Theatre. Do you want to walk up with her?'

He nodded. 'Yes, please. I'll come back down and talk to you later.'

Anna watched them go, then turned to Patrick. 'The horse was put down. I think the husband's relieved. The animal sounded like a menace.'

'Or just trying too hard to please,' Patrick said quietly. 'What a shame. Oh, well. Let's have a few ingrowing toenails to take the edge off that, shall we?'

Their next patient, however, was another casualty of sport, this time skiing.

'Skiing!' Patrick said. 'In May?'

'Dri ski-slope,' Anna told him. 'We quite often have them. He's done his thumb—typical skiing injury.'

Patrick nodded. 'Right. Let's see him.'

Anna called him into the cubicle, and Patrick gently examined his hand. The web of his thumb was very bruised and tender, and any movement of the thumb away from the palm was painful. The joint also appeared very unstable, and when Patrick asked him to hold a coin between his thumb and forefinger he dropped it, because he was unable to support the thumb.

'You've got a rupture of one of the main supporting ligaments in your thumb,' Patrick told him. 'We'll have to do an X-ray to see if there's any bony damage. If not you'll just have to have it in a cast for a while. If you have damaged the bone, it'll need surgery to reattach the bony fragment to give the ligament stability.'

'That's what they had to do before, with the other one,' he said heavily.

Patrick grinned at him. 'Do you know you're the second person in today who's done something again? Do you all enjoy the experience so much the first time that you can't wait to repeat it?'

The man laughed weakly. 'Hardly. It hurts like hell.'

'I'm sure.' Patrick filled in the X-ray request form, handed it to the man and sent him to have the plates done. When he returned it was found that he had no bony involvement, so Patrick mobilised the joint gently and Anna plastered it in position.

'Come back tomorrow for a plaster check,' Patrick told him, 'then again in a fortnight to see how you're doing. It'll be probably be on there for five to six weeks.'

'And I thought sport was supposed to be healthy,' Anna said drily as she stood beside Patrick washing her hands.

He laughed. 'You're joking. Ten minutes in here and you realise sport is the most unhealthy idea ever dreamed up!'

They shared a smile, and then Patrick glanced at his watch. 'You should be off now, shouldn't you?'

She nodded. 'Yes. Are you still on tonight?'

He shook his head. 'No. Greg Warren's on. I'll take the mobile, though, so they can contact me if necessary.'

He looked around them, then dropped a quick kiss on her lips. 'Don't go to bed without me.'

She was stunned. It was the first time he had indicated that he would definitely come round, and as such she had to view it as progress.

She went home with a little bubble of happiness round her heart, collected Flissy and picked up a take-away on the way home.

'Is it your birthday?' Flissy said in amazement.

'No, darling, I just felt like a treat for us,' Anna told her, feeling a twinge of guilt that she treated her little daughter so rarely that she must think it was a birthday.

They ate it in the garden, sitting by the fence under the shade of next-door's apple tree, because even at five-thirty the sun was still strong.

She put Flissy to bed and waited up for hours for Patrick, but finally at one o'clock she had to admit he wasn't coming. So much for progress.

She went to bed and cried herself to sleep, then at two the doorbell rang.

She went down, unsure how to greet him, and his face was grey and sick with worry.

'I'm sorry I didn't come earlier. I've been at the hospital,' he told her, his voice raw. 'My father's had a stroke.'

Her heart filled with sadness for him, and, reaching out, she drew him into the house and put her arms round him. He stood motionless for a moment, then his arms came up and he held her hard against his chest.

'Oh, God, Anna, he looked awful. He looked bad before, but this stroke—the whole of one side of his face has dropped, and he's paralysed all down his right side.'

'Oh, no,' Anna whispered. 'Has he lost his speech?'

Patrick nodded. 'Yes, and he's confused and terrified. I must go, I've got to get back to the hospital, but I wanted to tell you.'

Anna hugged him again. 'Give your mother my love and tell her I'm sorry. I'll see you tomorrow.'

He nodded. 'I may not be at work, but I'll be in the hospital. I'll keep you posted.'

She watched him go, helpless to do anything, and then made herself a drink and took it up to bed.

Poor George, how awful. And he had so enjoyed their time in the garden yesterday. Tears welled in her eyes, and she let them fall for a dear, kind man who had come to the end of the road. Let it be quick, she thought. Don't make them all suffer any more than they have to.

She slept eventually, and in the morning she took

Flissy to her childminder's a little early and then went to the hospital. George Haddon was in a medical ward, she was told, and Patrick was asleep in the duty doctor's room down the corridor from A and E.

She took him a cup of tea, and was appalled to see how drawn he looked.

'I rang the ward, your father's comfortable,' she told him.

His shoulders dropped, and she realised he'd been bracing himself for bad news. He slid up the bed and sagged against the headboard, his eyes closed. 'What a night,' he sighed. 'Mum looks awful. I'm worried about her.'

'I'll go and see her in a minute. I just wanted to check you were OK.'

He opened his eyes and searched her face, then patted the bed. 'Sit down. I need a hug.'

She slid her arms round him, pillowed her head on his chest and held him tight. His arms lay loosely round her, as if even hugging her was too much effort. She realised he was bone-weary, and had probably been getting up in the night to his father in recent weeks, as well as doing every third night at the hospital.

'Why don't you stay there and I'll go and see your mother?' she suggested, but he shook his head.

'No, I'll go up. Give me the tea, then I'll disappear.'

'Were you needed in the unit during the night?' she asked him while he drank it.

He nodded. 'They tried to contact Jack, but someone had had the bright idea that they should go away, of course.'

His smile was wry, and Anna pulled a face.

'I'm sorry. If only I'd kept my mouth shut——'

'Jack might have been a statistic by now. You're quite right; he shouldn't have the motorbike and he shouldn't go caving—especially not when he's upset and worried.'

'But you're shattered,' she said softly.

'I'll live.' His grim voice reminded her that his father might very well not.

She took the cup from him, subdued, and then left him to wash and dress while she checked out the situation in the department.

They were only slightly busy, and as soon as Jack and Kathleen arrived she slipped out and went up to the medical unit.

The sister there showed her to George Haddon's bed, and Anna noticed that the cot-sides were up and the curtains half-drawn.

He was lying down on one side, and at the sight of him Anna felt a great well of sadness. 'Hello, there,' she said gently, stroking his cheek, and he looked at her with blurred, unfocused eyes. 'What have you been up to? It was all that gardening we did on Sunday, wasn't it? Still, at least it's done. I'll finish the rest next week for you, OK?'

A flicker of recognition flared briefly in his eyes, and then was gone. Anna turned to Maggie and hugged her.

'I'm so sorry about this,' she said quietly. 'Just when he was doing so well at home.'

Maggie's eyes filled, not for the first time, Anna realised, and she pressed a hankie against her mouth and shook her head in denial.

'Patrick, why don't I take your mother for a drink while you sit with your father?' Anna suggested.

'I can't leave him,' Maggie said worriedly, her hands shaking. 'I have to be here, in case—in case. . .'

She trailed off, her voice cracking, and Anna put an arm round her and led her gently away. 'Come on,' she said soothingly. 'We'll go and have a cup of tea and you can have a good cry without him seeing you.'

She took her into the sister's office, asked the ward orderly to bring a cup of tea for her and then held her while she sobbed. 'I never thought I'd have to see him like this,' she said brokenly. 'I've lost him, Anna—he's gone. . .'

She pulled herself together after a little while, and managed to drink her tea, although her hands were very unsteady. Patrick popped his head round the door, his face worried.

'Is she OK?' he asked.

His mother nodded. 'Yes, of course,' she said a little raggedly. 'I'm just letting off steam. Patrick, go back to him, he mustn't be alone——'

'The doctors are there. They want a word with you.'

Anna stood up. 'I'll go back to A and E. Keep in touch, won't you? And if there's anything I can do, please ask.'

'I'll come and see you,' Patrick promised. 'Thanks.'

He gave her a brief kiss, and she left them with the doctors.

Jack and Kathleen were in the office when she went back down, and called her in.

'How are things?' Kath asked. 'Is he any worse?'

Anna shook her head. 'I don't think so. It looks a fairly minor stroke, really, but it's taken out his communications network.'

Jack sighed. 'What a damn shame. I wonder if he'll make it?'

'God knows,' Anna said heavily. 'He was confused enough before, without this.'

Kathleen eyed her strangely. 'Did you know him, then?'

She shook her head. 'Not till Saturday. I spent the weekend there.'

Kath's eyebrows shot up, and Anna laughed. 'Not like that. I nursed him because the agency nurse had the weekend off and they couldn't get a replacement.'

'So this is your fault?' Jack said with a little chuckle.

'Jack, don't be awful,' Kathleen reproached him, and he apologised.

Anna gave a little shudder. 'Don't you think it hasn't occurred to me? What on earth did I do wrong? Did I not move him enough, or let him sit for too long? Should he have had his legs up all the time, or only part of it? The list is endless.'

'And none of it's your fault.'

'This is, though.' Jack waved a cheque for six thousand pounds under her nose.

Anna's eyes widened. 'What's that for?' she asked.

'The bike.'

'You sold it!'

His grin was wry. 'Yes, I sold it. Kath thinks you're the greatest thing since sliced bread. I'm thinking of having you transferred to Siberia.'

Kath laughed. 'Ignore him, he's only crabby because he's given up smoking again.'

Anna smiled. 'I'm glad I can do some good, anyway. How was your break?'

'Lovely,' Kath said fervently. 'Just what we both needed, wasn't it, darling?'

'I don't know,' Jack said with a rueful laugh. 'A little sleep wouldn't have gone amiss!'

Kathleen blushed, and with a smile Anna left them alone. So they were honeymooning again, were they? It was better than being at daggers drawn.

It wasn't a busy day, fortunately, as Patrick only appeared briefly after lunch to tell them that his father seemed stable and he was taking his mother home for some sleep.

'I'll be back soon,' he promised them, but Jack sent him on his way.

'Come in tomorrow if things look stable still,' Jack said, and after a second's hesitation Patrick nodded.

'OK, but call me if there's a crisis.'

'We don't have crises,' Jack said calmly.

Kathleen and Anna snorted, and Patrick's mouth lifted in a faint smile.

'But if you do——' he persisted.

'We'll call you. Go home to bed, man. You look terrible. You'll frighten the patients.'

Anna walked him to the door, and once in the corridor outside the unit, he turned to her.

'I need you,' he said quietly.

He was standing two feet away from her, but the air between them was alive with longing.

'I need you, too,' she told him. 'I'm there, if you feel you can get away.'

'Not tonight. Perhaps tomorrow.'

She nodded, and with a small, tired wink, he turned and walked up the corridor. Her heart went with him.

It was two more nights before he came to her, and when she let him in she took one look at him and opened her arms. He walked into them, tugged her against his chest, and stood there while she held him in wordless comfort.

After a while he lifted his head. 'Could we have a cup of coffee? I need to talk.'

She made them two mugs of instant, and they settled down together on the sofa. For a long time he said nothing, but then he tipped his head back and stared at the ceiling.

'I can't bear it, Anna,' he said softly. 'He's so unhappy. He cries all the time, and there's nothing I can say to comfort him——'

His voice cracked, and for a second Anna thought he would cry and let the pain out of his system, but he fought it back down. 'It's terrible to watch him and be so helpless. Mum's devastated. I can't reach her——'

He smacked the coffee down, slopping it over his hand, and reached for her. She set her own mug down more carefully and went into his arms, holding him close as he fought the pain inside.

'I need you,' he breathed unsteadily. Getting to his feet, he pulled her up and went up to her room, stripping rapidly and dragging her into his arms.

'God, it's been so long,' he murmured as he drew her down on to the bed. 'Let me touch you.'

He peeled away her clothes, his hands fanning her hair out over the pillow and sifting it through his fingers.

'You're lovely. I can't get enough of you,' he muttered, and his lips traced a path of fire from her lips down to her breasts and back again.

She reached for him, her patience gone, and with a muffled cry he moved over her and buried himself deep inside her.

Their loving was almost violent in its intensity, but it needed to be to burn off the pain he felt inside, and at the end, when she sobbed out his name, it mingled in the air with his own hoarse cry of surrender.

CHAPTER TEN

PATRICK'S father came home at the end of the next week, in the care of an agency nurse as before, and as before, Anna spent the weekend helping with him.

His stroke had left him without speech, but still reasonably able to feed himself. Communication was more difficult, but with patience and plenty of time, he managed to make his basic needs understood. Some things, however, were too hard to communicate and sometimes frustrated him to tears. Saturday afternoon was one of those times.

Sympathetic to his exasperation, Anna spent a long time trying to work out what was the matter.

It was gloriously warm, and as before they were in the garden. Anna could see he was getting upset, but as far as she knew he was comfortable. Finally, having exhausted all the physical avenues of possible distress, she followed the direction of his eyes, and saw he was staring at the flowerbeds, the recently cleaned ground covered once again with tiny seedling weeds.

'Shall we do some more?' she asked him, and the crooked half-smile on his lips was her reward. With an answering smile, she wheeled him over to the bed she had started on before, and, finding some gloves, she quickly hoed off the small growth and then carried on down the bed with the fork, tugging out the larger, older weeds, talking to him as she worked.

'This little *potentilla's* a beauty,' she told him. 'I haven't seen one of this type before. You've got a lot of unusual plants. I wish I had a garden—I'll have to come and do yours, instead.'

He smiled again, a cross between a grin and a grimace, and she winked at him. 'Let's get this end finished, and we can have a nice cup of tea and plan the changes for the autumn before I start the next bit.'

They both knew he might not see the autumn, but his mouth twisted again. They would play along with the game together, he seemed to say. Anna bent her head back to the weeds so that he didn't see the moisture welling suspiciously like tears in her eyes.

They joined the others under the tree for tea a while later, and Flissy, after watching George for a minute, sidled up to him and slipped her hand into his.

'I'm sorry you've been ill,' she said kindly. 'I was ill once, I hated it.'

He smiled again, his throat convulsing, and Anna saw his eyes fill with tears. Oh, dear, he was going to start her off again next.

'Flissy, darling, have you given Toby a mint today?' Maggie said, distracting her, and the little girl shook her head. She wouldn't leave George's side, though, and when Anna had finished giving him his tea in a feeder cup, she turned to Flissy.

'Would you like to help pull up the weeds?' she asked her.

Flissy nodded, and, ignoring Patrick's and Maggie's looks of horror, Anna wheeled George back over to the next flowerbed and started loosening the soil with a hand-fork.

'Here, Fliss, can you pull up the weeds I've loosened? Only the ones I'm digging up, though. The others are flowers.'

'I can see that,' Flissy told her patiently, and then, with elaborate care, she lifted out each and every weed Anna had loosened.

'What a help! Isn't she good, George? We'll make a gardener of her yet.'

George smiled his twisted smile, and Anna could have sworn there was an indulgent twinkle in his eye.

She winked at him, and a few seconds later he winked back. Leaning over, she dropped a kiss on his hand where it lay on his knee, and went back to her gardening, her heart full.

Patrick's feet came into view, and he crouched down by Flissy. 'Want to have a ride on Toby?' he suggested.

She shook her head firmly. 'I'm helping Mummy,' she announced.

Patrick looked helplessly at Anna, and she smiled.

'We're fine—aren't we, George? We need our little helper.'

George nodded slowly, and Patrick stared at him in amazement.

'Patrick, relax,' she told him. 'We aren't doing any harm.'

'He never lets anyone touch it,' Patrick said quietly.

'Well, he is now. Go and wash up or something.'

Dismissed, Patrick wandered off across the garden and into his flat. Anna could feel him watching through the window, and once she lifted her head and smiled at him.

She didn't know if he had seen, but she thought so. After a while Flissy got bored.

'Look at my hands—yuck!' she said, splaying her plump little fingers out for George to see.

'Yuck, indeed. Go and find Patrick and ask him to help you wash them,' Anna instructed. 'Maybe he'll take you on the pony now.'

He did, after her hands were cleaned up, and later, once George was settled in bed downstairs and Flissy upstairs, he thanked Anna for her kindness to his father.

'He's looked happier all day than he's been since he

had the stroke,' he said, and Anna could hear the relief and gratitude in his voice.

'He loves his garden. He's enjoyed himself.'

'Because you talk to him as if he's a person. Mum finds it terribly hard because she can't bear it that he won't be able to reply. I try, but I get so choked it's hard to cheer him up.'

He gave a rueful smile, and Anna reached out her hand and took his in it, squeezing comfortingly. 'I find it hard, too, but it's much easier for me, because I'm not involved,' she told him.

'And because you're a good communicator and a good listener. You read people.'

She laughed without humour. 'You think so? I have trouble with you.'

'Me? I'm an open book!'

She regarded him seriously. 'No, you're not. You're full of mysteries and secrets. You hide your true self, for fear of being hurt. I know. I do it too.'

He looked away, awkward now. 'I don't mean to,' he said gruffly. 'It's just that there are some things too deep to talk about.'

She nodded. 'I know. If you ever want to, you know you can trust me, don't you?'

He squeezed her hand. 'Thanks.' Straightening up, he levered himself out of the settee and looked down at her. 'I think I'll turn in now. Busy day tomorrow.'

Go on, run, Anna thought. Just when I'm getting close. She wondered what it would take to make him open up.

The next few weeks were hectic in the department, although fortunately for Patrick his father seemed stable, and gradually Patrick relaxed around him, chatting more normally and learning not to say things that required a reply.

He also learned to read his father's unspoken messages, and Anna saw a quiet friendship build up between the two men which was precious to both of them.

At work, however, there was nothing quiet. They were into the harvesting season, with haymaking and early wheat combining, and it brought the usual resultant plethora of farming accidents.

One man was brought in with his right foot severed at the ankle by a rotovator. He had travelled the whole length of the field back to the farmhouse to call for help, and before the ambulance arrived he had wrapped the stump and ice-packed it.

When he arrived in the department he was in extraordinarily good condition, his pulse and blood pressure well within the normal range, to their amazement.

'How did it happen?' Patrick asked him as he slowly injected diamorphine for the pain.

'Lost my balance,' he said heavily. 'I put my foot out to save myself, straight into the blades. Could have been worse; I could have gone in head-first. Rum old choice to make, eh?'

Patrick shared a wry smile. 'You've done very well. You've shown great presence of mind, getting back to the house and calling us, and then ice-packing it. That probably saved your life.'

He snorted. 'Got no choice, had I? I looked at it, and I thought, Hell, where's my foot? I realised then I had to get help. The wife was out, too, so no way was she going to come looking for me. I did what I had to do.'

Patrick nodded. 'I don't suppose your foot was worth saving?'

He shook his head. 'No way. All chewed up and ploughed in by now, I expect. I left the machine running—didn't feel up to climbing into the tractor cab and turning off the ignition!'

'I don't suppose you did,' Anna said sympathetically. 'How's it feeling now?'

'Easing off a bit, thank God. I was starting to come to, you know? It was OK at first, once I'd got over the shock, but then it started to really get me just before I got home. Since then, well! They gave me some gas in the ambulance. That helped a bit.'

He was taken up to Theatre for a more surgically acceptable amputation, and Anna started clearing up the cubicle.

'He's been very lucky,' Patrick said to her. 'I suppose because of the precise shearing and twisting action of the machinery he got arterial spasm, and so he's hardly lost any blood. It could have been very much more serious.'

'I can't believe he did what he did.'

Patrick shrugged. 'As he said, he had no choice. A man's got to do——'

'What a man's got to do!'

They exchanged a smile.

'Oh, well, it makes a change from people coming in with eyelashes in their eyes, I suppose,' Patrick said with a grin, and headed off to his next patient.

Two weeks later they had another agricultural accident to contend with, but this one was quite different. A farm worker had fallen into the front of a combine harvester and was trapped by steel spikes which had penetrated his shoulder and upper arm. It would be hours before he could be removed, and Patrick and Anna were volunteered.

'You get all the fun,' Kathleen said with a laugh. Anna looked at the gentle swell of her abdomen and raised an eyebrow.

'You want to go?'

She shook her head. 'Thank you, no. I'd hate to spoil your day.'

It was a bumpy ride across the field, Patrick wincing as his father's car grounded on a rut.

'He'd kill me if he knew what I was doing to his car,' he said.

'I doubt it. In your position I have no doubt your father would have done exactly the same thing.'

Patrick shot her a grin. 'Do you know, I think you could be right?'

Ahead of them they could see the ambulance and fire crews milling round a huge yellow machine. Patrick pulled up beside them and they got out and ran towards the cluster of people.

'Hello, Doc,' the fire officer said, and they recognised him from the lorry-in-the-house incident. 'Young man trapped on steel spikes, half under the second auger. The ambulancemen are with him now, but it'll be ages before we can get him out.'

'How many ages?' Patrick asked, striding towards the casualty.

'Three hours? We've started dismantling the machine, but we'll need heavy-duty cutting equipment.'

'Is it on its way?' he asked, climbing over the spikes to reach the injured man.

'Yes—be here soon.'

'Let's hope it's soon enough,' Anna heard Patrick mutter under his breath. Then he was at the man's side.

After a brief exchange with the ambulancemen to establish what they had done, he asked Anna for an IV line and then struggled to find a vein.

'We couldn't get a vein,' the ambulanceman said. 'His blood pressure's dropped like a stone.'

'I'll have to find the vein in his ankle, or go in through an artery. I can't get to his neck.'

He bent down and spoke to the man, telling him what he was going to do. Entonox was playing over his face, but because of the crash in blood pressure they were unable to give him anything stronger until Patrick managed to boost his blood volume a little. Speed was, therefore, of the essence.

Anna cut away his trouser leg, prepared as clean a field as possible and laid a thick pad under his leg to make him more comfortable. 'Shouldn't someone try and get something under his face? That stubble looks awfully harsh and prickly,' she said to Patrick as he prepared the instruments he would need for the procedure.

He glanced round. 'Good idea. Can someone carefully get a pad under his head? A folded shirt will do.'

One of the bystanders, a fellow farmworker by the look of him, ripped off his T-shirt and scrambled over the machine.

'Dave? It's OK, mate, they're going to get you out in a tick,' he told their patient, and Anna could hear the guilt and worry in his voice. Had he been driving the machine? Very likely.

Patrick opened the skin on the inside of the man's ankle, disclosed the vein and even then had difficulty, because his legs were lying above his head and the blood was pooling in his trunk. Finally, however, Patrick managed to get the cannula in.

'At last,' he muttered. 'Right, we'll squeeze a few bags of Haemacel into him and see if he picks up.'

It took time, but eventually his vital signs recovered to the extent that Patrick risked a small injection of pethidine. There was a drop in pressure, but only slight, and the man's distress seemed a little eased, so Patrick gave him another small dose. There was no further drop in pressure, and this time the pain relief finally seemed more effective.

Even so, he was in a very awkward position, and Anna could imagine simply lying like that without the spikes would be painful enough.

Unable to do anything more useful for the time being, she picked her way carefully across the spikes and used a cool damp cloth to wipe the sweat off his face and away from his eyes.

'Thirsty,' Dave mumbled.

Anna looked at Patrick.

'He can suck a wet swab—nothing more.'

She nodded, and finding some plain water she wet a swab and held it to his lips. He sucked greedily on it, then she saw his throat work. After that he seemed to sleep for a moment or two, and Anna held his hand and watched as the firemen dismantled the machinery.

The first roller, the one supporting his legs, they managed to remove while Dave's legs were held up, and then very carefully lowered to the ground.

He groaned as they moved him, and Anna squeezed his hand and reassured him. 'Soon have you out,' she promised vainly.

The heavy cutting gear had arrived, and the roller above his head was cut away and lifted clear. Then and only then could they assess the extent of the damage.

His shoulder and the whole length of his right arm, stretched out behind him, were impaled on six-inch spikes of metal. Patrick chewed his lip. 'We'll have to take him in like that.'

The fire officer shook his head. 'Can't. The spikes are connected to a bar inside the roller, and we'll have to cut both. He won't be able to stand it. We can't do it without hurting him, and we can't lift it. It must weigh half a ton. He'll have to come off.'

'Right.' Patrick stood up. 'We'll need an anaesthetist. I'm not prepared to take him off there without.'

Anna, monitoring his blood pressure, turned to
Patrick. 'I think you're going to have to. His BP's
down to eighty over forty. I think his brachial artery
might have gone. The ground underneath him's
soaked.'

Patrick swore softly. 'Right, alert Theatre that he's
coming in. We'll clean up the spikes, and lift him
straight off in one go. It'll have to be quick, though.'

Anna could hear the man's scream echoing in her
head all the way back to the hospital. She drove
Patrick's car this time, and tried desperately to concen-
trate on what she was doing instead of on Dave's
terrible cries of pain as they had lifted him. Still, he
was on his way in now, the ambulance streaking ahead
of her, siren wailing.

She followed at a more sedate pace and parked the
car outside the unit in Patrick's slot.

Then she went in, to find Jack and Kathleen dealing
with the casualty.

'Where's Patrick?' she asked.

Jack looked grim. 'He's gone up to ITU. We were
just going to call him. His father's in — had a massive
stroke. He's not expected to survive.'

George Haddon was buried six days later in the church-
yard near his home. Anna went to the funeral, out of
respect not only for Patrick and his mother, but for the
man she and Flissy had grown to love.

Maggie was very dignified, her grief firmly held down
during the service, but at the graveside, as the coffin
was lowered, she turned, and Patrick wrapped her in
his arms and held her.

It was Patrick who watched as they lowered his

father into the ground, and Patrick who threw the first handful of soil on to the coffin.

Then he turned away, his arm around Maggie, and for the first time that day Anna saw his eyes.

They were like black holes into his soul, bleak and despairing, utterly desolate. Anna wept for him.

He came to her that night, very late, after the little street had settled, and without a word Anna held out her arms to him. His mouth crushed down on hers, his pain boiling right under the surface, his need for Anna as ever the only outlet for his emotions.

Anna led him to her room and held him as he poured out his pain and passion, and then afterwards she stroked his damp hair back from his beloved face and kissed him tenderly.

'I love you,' she told him softly.

He stiffened. 'No,' he said brokenly. 'No, Anna, you mustn't.'

'But I do. I have done for ages, and I think you love me, too.'

He rolled away from her, his eyes stark and filled with pain. 'No.'

'Why? Because you still love Isobel?'

Her words fell into the silence like stones into a pond, rippling out, shattering the veneer of control.

'Don't,' he whispered harshly. 'Leave her out of this.'

'I can't, Patrick. She's here with us, and she will be until you let her go.'

He swung his legs over the side and sat with his back to her, his shoulders heaving.

'I love her,' he grated.

Anna closed her eyes. How could she fight him?

Don't give up! she heard. Fight for him! Don't let him do this to you both!

She opened her eyes, filled with new courage, and reached out her hand, resting it lightly on his shoulder.

'Patrick, Isobel's dead. You have to let her go.'

He sucked in a harsh breath and she could see he was struggling with his emotions.

'I didn't say goodbye,' he said in a voice torn with pain. 'There was no time.'

'Then do it now. Go and say goodbye, and let her go. I love you, Patrick. I need you, and so does Flissy. I think you need us, too, but until you face this we can't move on.'

He turned to her, his face streaked with tears. 'I'm sorry,' he said gently. 'I didn't mean to hurt you.'

He took a huge breath, fighting back the grief that threatened to swamp him, and then pulled on his clothes. His face was tortured and Anna wanted to hold him, but instinct told her to let him go.

'Take care,' she said softly.

'I—I need to get out——'

He ran down the stairs and out through the front door, slamming it behind him, and Anna heard him gun the car and race down the street.

She gave him fifteen minutes, then went out and rang Maggie from the call-box up the road. 'Maggie, I'm sorry to trouble you, but is Patrick back?' she asked.

'Yes, he's just come in. He's in his flat.' Maggie's voice sounded clogged with tears, and Anna apologised for disturbing her. 'That's all right, Anna,' she said. 'I'm just glad he's got someone who cares.'

'I've upset him,' Anna confessed. 'I just wanted to make sure he was home safely.'

'Yes. Yes, he is. Anna, come and see me some time. I'd like to talk to you. Not now——'

She broke off, and Anna promised to visit her very soon. She put the phone down, went back to the house and checked Flissy, then made herself a drink and curled up in the sitting-room and cried her eyes out.

The next few days at work were very strange for Anna. Patrick had rung in and spoken to Jack. She didn't know what he'd said, but both Jack and Kathleen were very kind to her. It didn't do her any good. She kept dissolving into tears, and after a couple of days she realised she was grieving for Patrick's father, as well as worrying about Patrick.

Knowing that somehow made it easier to deal with.

She threw herself into her work, needing the routine to keep her sane, while she tried not to think about Patrick and what he was going through.

He had to do it, should have done his grieving for Isobel years ago. Perhaps grief at his father's death would be the key to open his heart and let the pain go.

Curiously it was Jack Lawrence who was the most sympathetic. Or perhaps not so curiously, as he had lost his son. For the first time he talked to Anna about it, and she realised just what he had faced when Kathleen had told him she was pregnant.

A loss like that one would never get over; she could see that now. However, as Jack said, that didn't mean you couldn't move on, given time and love.

'I've been given another chance at fatherhood, one I thought I'd never have,' he told her quietly. 'It makes me proud and scared and ridiculously protective—I think I'm driving Kath mad.'

Anna smiled faintly. 'I don't doubt it. Are you really reconciled to the baby now?'

He grinned. 'Reconciled? Anna, I'm ecstatic. I loved my son—loved being a father. It was wonderful, in the good bits. Even in the bad bits I could never regret it. That's the hardest thing about love. It opens you up to all sorts of hurt, and once you've learned that, you tend to fight shy of involvement in case it hurts again. After all, if you don't love, you can't hurt.'

And that, she realised, was what Patrick was running from. She wasn't sure if that gave her hope or not.

Five days after the funeral she went and saw Maggie.

'Patrick's not here,' she told Anna.

Anna tried not to be disappointed. 'That's all right,' she told Maggie. 'We've come to see you, anyway. How are you?'

'I'll do.'

She was calm and composed, but obviously very sad. 'I've been grieving for him for ages, of course,' she told Anna as they sat in the conservatory watching Flissy playing with the kittens. 'I think I lost my husband a long time ago.'

Anna nodded. 'Yes, maybe you did, and in another way, maybe you never will.'

They shared a sad smile. Anna, fiddling with her glass, glanced across the garden at Patrick's flat.

'How is he?' she asked softly.

'Patrick? I think he'll be all right. He took his father's death very hard, but I think there was more to it. I think it was all tied up with Isobel.'

Anna nodded. 'I told him to say goodbye.'

'Ah.' Maggie smiled. 'He's gone to Scotland. Her ashes are there—at the top of Ben Nevis. That's where he'll be. Funny, he's never been back since the day he took her ashes up there alone.'

'Will he be all right?' Anna asked, suddenly fearful.

Maggie squeezed her hand. 'He'll make it. Just hang on.'

'I hope you're right,' Anna murmured.

'You love him very much, don't you?'

Her heart contracted. 'More than I can say. I just hope it's enough.'

It was beautiful at the top of the mountain, a clear, cloudless day just like the day when Patrick had walked up there with Isobel and their team of supporters.

She had nearly killed herself doing it, he remembered, but she was never one to be thwarted. 'I'm going to walk up Ben Nevis,' she had announced after watching a documentary on Scotland.

'Don't be daft,' he'd said.

He hadn't known her very long then. They'd only been married six months.

She went into training, forcing her legs to carry her round and round their flat, going out for walks without her chair, tackling stairs which were too much for her, until in the end she announced she was ready.

Patrick, unconvinced, gathered a party of strong friends and they set off at six o'clock one clear day in June. The weather was brilliant, and so was Isobel. Stubborn, pig-headed—she redefined the words.

And when ten hours later she got to the top, she'd thrown back her head and laughed until the mountains rang with her delight.

'Oh, it's so beautiful up here,' she said to Patrick. 'When I die, I want my ashes scattered here so I can look at it for ever.'

Patrick glanced at his watch. 'Yes, and if we don't get you down soon, that might be quicker than you think,' he told her with a smile.

'Oh, poo. I've come all this way—let me sit for a minute.'

So they had, taking photos of the party and the spectacular views across the hills to Loch Linnhe bathed in gold by the afternoon sun, and then Patrick had lifted her in his arms and carried her, protesting, down the mountain.

'I can walk!' she declared.

'I don't doubt it, but we need to get down in daylight,' he said drily. 'Besides, you may be all right, but the rest of us are starving!'

They took it in turns to carry her, he remembered, and by the time they got down they were all exhausted. She had done it, though, succeeded where everyone had thought she would fail.

The echo of her laughter came back to him, and he smiled at the memory.

'I miss you,' he told her quietly. 'Life's been pretty grim since you went. I've met someone else, now, though. I think you'd like her. She's not as pushy as you, but she's got guts in her way.' A smile played around his lips. 'She's got a little girl who reminds me of you, with a stubborn chin and naughty, twinkling eyes. I think she's going to be quite a handful to bring up, one way and another.'

He twisted his wedding-ring on his finger. 'Anna told me to come and say goodbye, to let you go. I didn't think I could, but maybe it's time now. I won't forget you, though. You brought sunshine into my life, and laughter, and you'll always have a very special place in my heart——'

He broke off, staring out over the hills and valleys, and, twisting off his ring, he hefted it in his hand.

'It's time to move on now. I've got a new life waiting. I hope you're happy, wherever you are, giving the angels hell.'

A sad smile touched his mouth, and, lifting the ring to his lips, he kissed it, and lobbed it over the side of the mountain, down the ravine where her ashes lay.

As he turned a man approached him cautiously, his eyes concerned.

'Are you OK, mate?'

Patrick nodded. 'Yes—yes, I am,' he said, suddenly realising it was true. 'I was just saying goodbye to someone.'

'Must have been a hell of a friend,' the man said.

Patrick smiled. 'She was.'

Turning, his heart suddenly lighter, he made his way back down the mountain.

He was going home.

Anna was working in the garden when she felt her skin prickle. Seconds later she heard his car, then footsteps on the gravel.

She stood up, tugging off her gloves, and brushed her hands down her ancient jeans. Her palms felt damp and clammy, but whether from the gloves or because Patrick was here, she didn't know.

He came through the kitchen door and his eyes found her instantly. Slowly, as if he didn't want to startle her, he moved forward.

'Hi.' His voice was gruff, but the terrible haunted look in his eyes was gone.

She allowed herself a faint smile of greeting. It was all she could manage, because her heart was thrashing like a wild thing and she knew her whole life pivoted on the next few minutes.

'Hi,' she murmured.

'I went to your house, but you weren't there. I guessed you'd be here.'

Her heart jerked. He had come to find her! Surely, then——?

'I went to Scotland.'

'I know. Your mother told me.'

'To say goodbye to Isobel.' He held out his hand to her. The ring was missing, a stark white band where it had been. She moved forward until their fingers meshed.

'Are you OK?' she asked him.

He smiled tenderly. 'Yes—yes, I'm OK. I realised something up there. I don't have to stop loving her, just because I love you now. She'll always be special, but she's gone. You were right, it was time to let her go. I can't forget her, though,' he added, almost as if he was warning her.

'I wouldn't expect you to. I wouldn't want to be forgotten.'

'No.' He stepped closer, so that Anna could feel the heat of his body warming the cold fear around her heart. 'You see, I realised that we aren't just given a certain amount of love. I don't have to stop loving Isobel just because I love you. We have enough love in our hearts for all our needs. It isn't measured, counted out like coins. It's like a wellspring that never runs dry, and we've all got it—more than enough, love without measure.'

His knuckles brushed her cheek. 'And I do love you. I had trouble sorting that out, because I felt so guilty about Isobel, but I don't any more. I can still have my memories, and my love for her still counts, even though it's lost.'

His hand cupped her face, his thumb softly caressing her cheek. 'I love you, Anna—you and Flissy. It's time to move on, to start my life again. Let me do that with you—share my life, Anna. Give me back my sunshine.'

Her eyes filled. 'Oh, Patrick,' she cried, and, throwing herself into his arms, she hugged him and wept.

'Anna?' he said worriedly. 'Darling, don't cry—oh, God, please, tell me what's wrong.'

She lifted her head and smiled through her tears. 'Nothing's wrong, idiot! I'm just happy! I love you!'

Relief flooded his face, and, hugging her against his

chest, he swung her round, his laughter echoing round
the sunlit garden, filling her heart.

'Patrick! Patrick, you're home!'

Little feet came pounding towards them, and, releas-
ing Anna Patrick swept Flissy up into his arms, pressing
a smacking kiss to her cheek, before putting her down
again to take Anna back in his arms.

Flissy looked up at him, then at her mother. 'You've
made Mummy cry,' she said accusingly.

Anna smiled at her daughter. 'I'm happy, that's
why.'

'Are you going to marry Mummy?' Flissy asked with
childish directness.

Anna held her breath, but Patrick released her and
crouched beside Flissy. 'I haven't asked her yet. Would
you like me to?'

Flissy nodded. 'You'd better. She can be funny about
it if you don't ask if you can do something first.'

His mouth quirked, stifling the grin. 'Can she? I'll
have to remember that.' He straightened up and met
Anna's breathless look, his love clear in his warm
brown eyes. 'So, Anna, will you marry me, and let me
look after you and Flissy?'

'Of course I'll marry you,' she said unevenly, and as
he pulled her back into his embrace the tears began to
fall again.

'You'll have to stop making her cry,' Flissy said
thoughtfully.

Anna sniffed and tried to pull herself together. 'I'm
fine, really. Just happy. . .'

Flissy gave her a disbelieving look, then switched her
attention back to Patrick. 'Can we live here? If we
don't, Toby will miss us.'

Patrick smiled. 'It's up to your mother. She may not
want to live here with my mother.'

'Why ever not?' Flissy asked, amazed.

'Yes, why ever not? I love your mother,' Anna told him simply.

Patrick eyed her thoughtfully. 'Do you mean that? It's one of the things that's been worrying me, because they were talking of selling up and moving to something more manageable. If we were here, we could cope with it together. And my mother could look after Flissy until she starts school in September.'

'Oh, I wouldn't dream——'

'Wouldn't dream of what? Is this private or can anyone join in?'

Patrick turned to include his mother in the conversation, his smile rueful. 'I'm glad you're here. I was just planning your life for you.'

She smiled. 'Oh?'

'How would you feel about Anna and Flissy moving in? And looking after Flissy while Anna's at work—just until the next one comes along, of course.'

Anna gasped. 'The next one?'

'Don't you want another baby?'

She met his open gaze, and saw the yearning deep in his heart. 'Of course I do,' she said, a smile dawning in her eyes.

'I hope you intend to marry her first,' Maggie said drily.

'Of course,' they chorused.

Anna saw the sadness recede a little in Maggie's eyes. 'I think it all sounds wonderful.'

'So do I,' Anna murmured, and then her wretched eyes filled again. 'Oh, damn. . .'

'You've made her cry again,' Flissy said accusingly.

'I'm happy,' she sniffed.

Flissy pulled a face and peered at Patrick. 'Are you crying too?' she said in disgust.

He laughed, and scooped Flissy up into his arms. 'Of course not.'

She stared into his suspiciously bright eyes and sniffed. 'Maybe Mummy wants a ride on Toby to cheer her up?'

'Poor Toby,' Anna said, with a shaky little laugh.

'Maybe she just wants a big hug from all of us,' Patrick suggested.

As their arms closed around her, wrapping her in three generations of love, Anna couldn't think of a single thing she would rather have. . .

MILLS & BOON

KIDS & KISSES

Kids & Kisses—where kids and romance go hand in hand.

This summer Mills & Boon brings you Kids & Kisses— a set of titles featuring lovable kids as the stars of the show!

**Look out for
Fire Beneath the Ice by Helen Brooks
in August 1995**

Kids...one of life's joys, one of life's treasures.

Kisses...of warmth, kisses of passion, kisses from mothers and kisses from lovers.

In Kids & Kisses...every story has it all.

MILLS & BOON

are proud to present...

A set of warm, involving romances in which you can meet
some fascinating members of our heroes' and heroines'
families. Published each month in the Romance series.

Look out for "Make-Believe Family" by Elizabeth Duke
in August 1995.

Family Ties: Romances that take the family to heart.

FREE

Return this coupon and we'll send you 4 Love on Call novels and a mystery gift absolutely FREE! We'll even pay the postage and packing for you.

We're making you this offer to introduce you to the benefits of Reader Service: FREE home delivery of brand-new Love on Call novels, at least a month before they are available in the shops, FREE gifts and a monthly Newsletter packed with information.

Accepting these FREE books and gift places you under no obligation to buy, you may cancel at any time, even after receiving just your free shipment. Simply complete the coupon below and send it to:

HARLEQUIN MILLS & BOON, FREEPOST, PO BOX 70, CROYDON, CR9 9EL.

No stamp needed

Yes, please send me 4 free Love on Call novels and a mystery gift. I understand that unless you hear from me, I will receive 4 superb new titles every month for just £1.99* each postage and packing free. I am under no obligation to purchase any books and I may cancel or suspend my subscription at any time, but the free books and gifts will be mine to keep in any case. (I am over 18 years of age)

2EP5D

Ms/Mrs/Miss/Mr _____

Address _____

_____

_____ Postcode _____

Offer closes 31st January 1996. We reserve the right to refuse an application. *Prices and terms subject to change without notice. Offer only valid in UK and Ireland and is not available to current subscribers to this series. **Readers in Ireland please write to: P.O. Box 4546, Dublin 24.** Overseas readers please write for details.

You may be mailed with offers from other reputable companies as a result of this application. Please tick box if you would prefer not to receive such offers. ☐

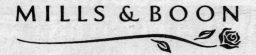

MILLS & BOON

LOVE ON CALL

The books for enjoyment this month are:

LOVE WITHOUT MEASURE	Caroline Anderson
VERSATILE VET	Mary Bowring
TARRANT'S PRACTICE	Abigail Gordon
DOCTOR'S HONOUR	Marion Lennox

Treats in store!

Watch next month for the following absorbing stories:

MIDWIFE'S DILEMMA	Lilian Darcy
MADE FOR EACH OTHER	Elizabeth Harrison
HOSPITAL AT RISK	Clare Lavenham
SEEING EYE TO EYE	Josie Metcalfe